Simmering, Savory, and Deadly: A Soup Makers Mystery
Copyright © 2023 Jody Rich

ISBN: 978-1-63381-377-9

All rights reserved. No part of this book may be reproduced in any form or by any electronic or mechanical means, including information storage and retrieval systems, without permission in writing from the author, except by a reviewer, who may quote brief passages in review.

This is a work of fiction. Names, characters, places, and incidents either are the product of the author's imagination or are used fictitiously, and any resemblance to actual persons, living or dead, is coincidental.

Cover illustration by Laura Lander
Author photo by Gale Davison

Permissions
"Spirit of Life." Copyright © 1981 Surtsey Publishing,
renewed © 1993 Carolyn McDade.
Used by permission; all rights reserved.

Designed and produced by:
Maine Authors Publishing
12 High Street, Thomaston, Maine
www.maineauthorspublishing.com

Printed in the United States of America

Simmering, Savory, and Deadly

A Soup Makers Mystery

Jody Rich

Chapter One

I smiled. The tea kettle was whistling and I could hear my wife, Brie, bustling to the stove to pour our morning tea. I lingered between the toasty sheets. She would have the cat fed, the dishwasher emptied, and the newspaper grabbed from the back stoop before I put my feet on the floor. I shrugged off the covers, opened the bedroom door, and hollered out, "Good morning."

"Good morning, Vidalia. Snow is falling and everything is being cancelled."

"Snow Day!" I yelled. Since I retired from public education, every snowy day could be a snow day, but an actual one was still special. We live in the middle of Maine, and it *was* January. Of course we were having more snow.

"Something different," I responded with my usual sarcasm. "I'll be out in a sec." I pulled on my robe and shoved my feet into well-loved sheepskin-lined slippers.

Brie stood in front of the double glass doors leading to our deck. "It looks like another fifteen inches."

She shivered as she handed me my steaming cup of green tea with honey. Brie comes from good French-Canadian stock. She is petite and rounded; that pillowy-softness on the outside buffers the ruggedness inside. A former athlete, she is still more muscle than anything else and is almost always warm.

I took a sip and shivered. "I get a chill just looking out the window. At least we don't have to be dressed and headed out to work in this. When I think about you heading Downeast to meet with constituents for the congressman just as it started snowing here. Or when you would head out to the political group in Belfast just ahead of some of these storms. What were we thinking?"

"We weren't thinking. We were working." Brie bumped her hip against mine and continued. "How many times did you arrive at a school for an early special education meeting and find the parking lot hadn't been plowed? That was your first hint that school had been cancelled."

"Didn't that burn my butt." I chuckled. "I would half-freeze before the car warmed up just getting there. After I cussed about having a perfectly good work outfit go unused, I would head to the nearest diner and have breakfast."

I come from Irish and Scottish descent. I describe myself as the runt of the litter among my siblings. I'm the smallest-boned and the shortest. My feet are often freezing cold, even in summer. I wear turtlenecks three seasons of the year. My teeth chatter in a cool breeze. I run chilled.

I put one arm around Brie's warm, cushioned waist. She put one hand on my bony shoulder. We both sipped and looked out at the falling snow.

"Our days of keeping an overnight bag in the trunk of our cars are over," I said.

"And don't forget having enough money on our credit cards to afford an unplanned motel room if a storm hit while we were there," Brie said. "Now we can just stay home."

"But this," I swept my arm toward the windows, "is an endurance test." After a few more sips and sighs, I added, "Let's see if we can change our perspective with a visualization."

"You and your visualizations. If you can change my wet, slushy mood, I'll be grateful. Give it your best shot."

"Okay," I started. "Take a sip of tea and feel it warming your insides. Take a calming breath."

We closed our eyes and breathed. We stood with our feet shoulder width apart.

"In your mind's eye, turn all this snow into warm, white sand. These are dunes in the Caribbean, maybe our favorite San Mar-ten," I said with my best but still terrible French accent. Brie is fluent, so any attempt on my part is encouraged, but this made her giggle.

I continued. "Imagine that drainpipe coming down the side of the house as a palm tree. Let large, green palm leaves extend over some of this sand right in front of us."

"I think I see a coconut," Brie smiled, taking another air-rippling sip of her tea.

"Yes!"

The wind whipped around the house, and our eyes flew open. Snowflakes swirled. It hissed at us as it hit the glass. We both shuddered, but I wasn't giving up.

"Hear that wind? Let it make the palm leaves and coconuts sway."

"That's stretching it, Vidalia," Brie quipped. "I see snow, not sand, and I see a drainpipe, not a tree."

She turned to me with a twinkle in her eye. "Why are we visualizing it when we could be there? We're retired. Let's go get warm."

"I am on it!" I headed to the computer.

Within the hour, I had traded our timeshare in Ellsworth for a week in Saint Martin. A quick session with an online travel agency, we had round-trip tickets.

I announced to Brie, "Done. We leave in three weeks."

We heard our plow gal clearing the driveway.

"Perfect timing." I smiled. "Let's go out for breakfast to celebrate and plan. I'll call my sister to join us. Maybe Olive can take care of the cat while we're gone."

I drove cautiously to Eric's, a family-owned and operated restaurant close by. I felt proud to see the number of cars and trucks in the parking lot. There's nothing like a good storm to get Mainers out and about.

No stinkin' snow was gonna keep us home.

As we were settling in at our table, Olive came in flapping snow off the hood of her down jacket.

"It took me a while to get out. I had to shovel through what the city plow left behind at the end of my driveway. I worked up a sweat, for cryin' out loud. It's wicked out there."

Olive is taller and bigger-boned than I am. She is the tallest one in our family. Living in Vermont's Northeast Kingdom for several years, she developed muscles, grit, and endurance to get through anything. She pulled out a chair and sat down. She smiled to the waitress for her usual hot tea with milk.

"Guess where I'm going?" she asked us, all smiles.

"Where?" I asked.

"To Saint Martin. Isn't that one of your favorite places to go? Coco is a great one for finding nursing conferences in warm places so she can get out of Alaska for a while. She found one about using local herbs and remedies, and she's always working with herbalists and natural healers in the more remote villages she goes into. So, I'm going for fun and I'll get to see what you like about it while she's at her conference. It's on some nearby island."

"Saba," Brie and I said at the same time. We sat back in our chairs. The waitress brought our hot drinks.

"What?" Olive asked.

Brie asked, "When exactly are you going to meet this longtime friend of yours?"

"In about three weeks."

Brie's eyes popped.

"Maybe I'll find a new soup recipe for Rachel's restaurant. I'm so excited to get out of this cold I hadn't even thought about that." She rubbed her hands together. "My time off is already approved. I'll need to reschedule my Body Safety lessons in the schools, but it's worth it. Co-workers will cover my Parenting classes at the jail." She looked at us just sitting there looking at her. "What-a?"

"It just so happens that Brie and I are going to Saint Martin in three weeks," I said.

Olive's eyes widened, and she started to smile even broader than before.

"I just made our arrangements," I continued. "We're here to celebrate and plan."

I tore off a third of my paper placemat and turned it over for note-taking.

"We thought you might take care of the cat, but I guess you will be otherwise engaged." I smiled at her.

"I'll call the cat-sitting lady when we get home," Brie said and started a list on the iPad she had brought with her. At our house, if it isn't written down, it's not going to get done.

We are a list-making people.

A customer in a parka with a fur-trimmed hood and serious mittens came in, stamping snow off his insulated LL Bean boots.

"Snow's turnin' to ice, folks. Eat up," he announced as he headed for a stool at the counter. "The hottest coffee you've got, please. I'll be saltin' and sandin' for the duration so I'm gonna fill myself up now. I expect every place will be closin' down shortly." He eased onto a stool and mumbled loud enough to be heard by the owner, "Should be, anyway."

"Ice," I said. "That's the worst. I'm glad we live close by. Let's order."

Brie and I split a spinach, artichoke, and feta omelet. Olive had one poached egg with a single slice of raisin toast. She snagged an artichoke heart off my plate.

"So," I began, "when exactly are you going? Which airline and out of which airport?" I had pen in hand, and Brie started tapping on her iPad.

Olive gave me her deadpan look that she's been giving me all of our lives.

"You know I have no idea what the answers are to any of those questions, Vidalia. None." She sipped her tea. "I just found out I'm going the other day. It's all in my computer and I have electronic tickets so I can't possibly lose them." She looked at me knowingly.

She's misplaced an important piece of paper or two over the years.

She continued, "You know my Kate Ann is on it like sand on a beach." She paused for a beat. "Did you like what I did there? We're going to a beach."

We gave her a pity laugh.

"Anyway, I'm grateful I have a child who became a travel agent. All of that searching and comparing makes me tense. I *do* know that I fly out of Boston straight to Saint Martin and that's supposed to be a great thing," she said. "Coco will have to leave three days earlier just to get there on time. Geesh, living in Alaska has its price, but she is probably even more excited than we are to get someplace hot. She's reserved a room at some resort. La-di-dah. I can't wait."

She took a bite of her toast, sat back, closed her eyes, and savored the tastes and possibilities. "Cinnamon and butter…warm, rich, and spicy; just perfect."

"Well," Brie said, "let's coordinate our details and find out if we can travel together. It would be fun to share our love of Saint Martin with you."

"Do you want me to email Kate Ann for the details, Olive?" I asked. "Have you told your other kids? I'll bet Micah and Anna are thrilled for you. And what do we need to do so Rachel's pizzeria doesn't suffer while we're gone?"

Olive looked at Brie and raised one eyebrow, then she turned to me with a look of warning. "You are so organized, Vidalia. Can't we just think about the trip?" She took a swallow of tea and sighed but continued.

"Yes, all of my children know," Olive said. "I'll make up enough soup and freeze it so Grand Pizza has plenty while I'm gone. Desserts aren't as good after they've been frozen so Rachel will either make the carrot cake herself or order from someone. Anna will do the laundry."

Olive's face changed. Instead of answering *my* questions, she became the investigator.

"What are you going to do about your end of things? Surely, you have a list," she said, trying to get to me.

While she had been blah-blah-blahing, I had been jotting things down.

I raised a finger for each item as I read them. "Get plenty of cash and change for the safe; pay all bills up to date; get someone to take care of the recycling." I raised my eyes up, clicked the pen closed, and looked at Olive over the top of my eyeglasses.

"You're such a jerk," she said, laughing.

"Someone has to be," I replied.

Chapter Two

The next three weeks were full of snow and sleet. My remedy was to stroke my bathing suit and speak gently to it.

"It won't be long now, dear, and pretty soon we'll be floating in the warm ocean.

Before you know it, we'll be stretched out on a chaise lounge under a palm tree!"

I emailed Kate Ann for Olive's travel arrangements.

"We lucked out," I said to Olive when I saw her next. "We have the same airlines, flights, and times so we can travel together."

Olive and I ensured that Grand Pizza wouldn't suffer from our absence. She made up extra soups each week and put them in the freezer. The linens would be laundered by Anna, who also waited tables part-time at the Grand. Rachel contacted a trusted vendor for desserts to be baked and delivered.

I stocked the safe with enough coins and bills to avoid a trip to the bank, left materials in the safe so someone could make a cash deposit, and spent time with one of the other bakers Tim, an Earth-lovin' hippie at heart, to cover the recycling.

Brie called the cat sitter and the snow plow gal. She let the veterinarian know that we would be traveling and that Brie would be responsible for any emergencies for our cat once we returned. She stacked hard and canned cat food, treats, and litter to last well beyond our time away on the kitchen counter. Finally, she contacted the credit union to make them aware of our traveling.

On travel day, she topped off all of her seven bird feeders and left the bags and barrels in the entryway for the cat sitter for refilling as needed.

I drove the three of us down to Portland. We took the bus from there to Logan airport and flew directly to Saint Martin. What a coup that was. A nonstop flight that we could afford. The flight was fun. I enjoy celebrating whenever I can, so as soon as the flight attendants were taking drink orders, I ordered.

"Two mimosas, please," indicating Brie and myself.

"Those are not complimentary in coach, you know."

I knew.

"Getting out of the snow and heading to warmth is cause for celebration," I explained with a face full of sincere excitement and anticipation in my eyes.

She delivered. Reaching across Brie in the aisle seat, she handed me the single-serving bottle of champagne and a cup of orange juice. Then she served Brie the same. I clapped my hands in glee.

Olive's hot tea was carefully handed across both of us to the window seat.

"To us!" I toasted. "To easy travel and the promise of opportunities we haven't even dreamt of yet."

"Like a new soup recipe," Olive chimed in.

We clinked cups. "Hear, hear," chorused Olive and Brie. We attracted a few happy glances from nearby travelers.

For our in-flight meals, Brie and I ordered one meat and one vegetarian so we could pick and choose from each.

"Too bad they don't serve a soup," Olive said over her vegetarian dish.

"Hot soup in an airplane in the middle of the air. Doesn't sound like a safe option," Brie answered.

"You've got a point there, Brie," Olive conceded. "But a few spoonfuls of something warm and savory would taste good right now."

"Soup is more than just the ingredients to you, isn't it?" Brie asked.

Olive put her fork down on her tray. "For me, soup-making has a deeper meaning. Our mom's mom, Nana, made soup."

"I remember sitting at her kitchen table," I added.

"'Knees under the table at noon,' we air quoted one of Nana's sayings in unison.

"Nana would ladle out a bowlful." Olive gazed out the window and came back to us. "It was the very best, ever. She used those wide egg noodles. And lots of celery, onion, and more carrots than anything else. Her leftover roasted chicken went into the pot whole, so all the goodness seeped out of the bones. She didn't use a lot of salt, either." She closed her eyes for a moment.

"I always wished that someday I could make soup as good as hers." I met my sister's eyes and gave her a big warm hug of a smile.

"Every once in a while," Olive said as she lifted her spoon and stirred her tea, "I feel like I've hit that sweet spot while cooking at the restaurant—that Nana would be happy with my soup."

Brie said, "I didn't get to know your Nana or her soups, but I like all of yours. I'm pretty sure you are carrying on her legacy." She drank the last of her mimosa.

"Her legacy," I said. "I hadn't thought of it that way. I like the idea of you remembering Nana with respect and carrying on her soup-making."

Our eyes watered for a few seconds even as we smiled.

Making a stab at humor, I said, "Nana wouldn't like this airplane or the food at all."

"Heck no," Olive answered. "All the hustle and bustle and waiting? She would be silent and ugly." Olive made the disapproving face Nana used to make, sticking out her bottom lip and dropping her chin. Her eyes looking downward as if closing the world out. We chuckled at the thought.

After the food and dinnerware were cleared away, we fell into reading books. In time, the pilot came on the intercom.

"Good afternoon, ladies and gentlemen. We will begin our descent into Princess Julianna Airport, Saint Martin, in a few minutes. With a tailwind, we are a little ahead of schedule. Saint Martin is enjoying a mild eighty-two degrees with a slight breeze. Enjoy the rest of your flight."

I clapped in glee. I'm a gleeful person whenever the opportunity presents itself.

Olive looked out the window. "The clouds are getting thinner, and I can see the ocean way down below. Oh my goodness, this is really happening." She smiled, keeping watch out the window and giving updates as details came into view.

"Oh! I can see the island! It's like a postcard."

We heard the pilot. "Welcome to Saint Martin, ladies and gentlemen. Thank you for flying with us today. Please remain seated with your seatbelts fastened until the aircraft comes to a complete stop at the gate."

The unclicking of seatbelts could be heard all over the plane.

After deplaning, we made a beeline to the bathrooms. Let's agree that airplane bathrooms are not conducive to a relaxing pee. Then we scurried to Baggage Claim. That section of the airport was not air-conditioned, and the heat and humidity hit us like a warm, wet blanket. We changed from sneakers to sandals and headed for the taxi stand.

Chapter Three

Our taxi driver took the luggage out of his van in front of the reception area at the resort. We could hear beach party music so I started swaying while paying him.

He smiled, "You are already in the island spirit!"

"Oh yes." I smiled back.

We walked inside the lobby and could see directly across to the quadruple-width sliding glass doors opening out to the beach and beautiful ocean. And there, standing within that doorway, was Coco. The sun shone through her red hair with gray highlights, as she called them, making her look like a well-proportioned tropical fairy. She was waiting for us in a Hawaiian-print shirt and red shorts with red sparkle flip-flops, all in extra-large sizes. She came at us, squealing with happiness, arms outstretched for a group hug. Coco's personality was bigger than she was.

"Isn't this great?" she said. "I've been here long enough to shower and change clothes. I want to spend the whole time here outside. I can feel my body melty-relaxing. I hadn't realized how scrunched up I was trying to stay warm in Alaska."

"This is great," Olive agreed. She looked around the lobby and out onto the beach. "Let's get checked in so we can change clothes. I want to walk on that beach!"

Coco said, "We're already checked in. Here's your key. I'll go up with you to dump your stuff."

"Okay," I said. "We'll check in and bring our suitcases up to our unit and meet you back here."

"How about we meet out on the patio?" Brie offered.

"Yes!" we said in unison.

Brie and I went to the reception desk and received a warm and friendly welcome. Along with our unit keys, the clerk handed us a folder of the resort's weekly activities and several colored flyers for special events. We also noticed posters for an event that evening. Brie asked about it.

"This evening, we are hosting 'A Night Out for the Kids,' a fundraising gala for our island orphanage. Some of the children will be performing. There will be other wonderful performers as well as dinner and music. How many tickets would you like?"

Brie and I looked at each other, nodded in assent, and turned to the clerk.

"We'll take four tickets, please," said Brie. "This will be my first fun purchase while we're here. It's for a good cause, and the four of us can go together."

"Nice! Thank you, Brie," I said.

We went up in the elevator and got into our unit with a mere three tries with the electronic key. We opened the sliding door to the balcony and breathed deeply.

"Honey, we're here in paradise," I said, stepping over to the railing. "We made this happen. Thanks for a wonderful suggestion."

Brie came out and made a huge stretch. Her arms out to the sides and then swung up over her head. She flopped them downward and bent at the waist. She came back upright and took a long, slow breath.

"God, that felt good," she said, walking over to me.

Arms around each other's waists, she said, "I want to walk the beach at least once a day and I mean more than two-minute walks. What about you?"

"I plan to swim every day. I want this body buoyant. I want these muscles stretched out but no pain or sweat," I answered. "What else?"

Brie thought and said, "I want to listen to people speaking French and understand it. I want to read the newspaper and understand it. I want to speak French and have a real conversation about something more than menu items."

"Wow, I just want to avoid a sunburn. While you're doing all that, I'll people-watch and make up stories."

I brushed my fingers through her hair and said, "I want to sit in the shade and relax with you, each with a book and a tall glass of iced tea. I want us to not think about home or anyone or anything there. Let's act like jet-setters without a responsibility in the world. How's that sound?"

"Whew!" Brie giggled. "I like the sound of that, with a few alterations. You can sit in the shade and I'll be in the sun. You read a book and I'll read a newspaper. I'll join you on that iced tea, though."

I kissed her on the cheek. "Got it. Let's make this happen."

We went back inside, unpacked our bags, and put things away. When our temporary home was set up, we went down to the patio.

Chapter Four

The lobby and patio areas were bustling. Staff were setting up tables with chairs and linens, extra lighting, and food-holding equipment. Others were bringing in sound and musical equipment. The piped-in beach party music gave a light and festive feel to the commotion. There was a rolling rack of what must have been costumes for the performance. I walked over to it.

"Brie, look at these colors and fabrics. Aren't they wonderful? The skirts are voluminous, and those solid crayon-box colors are vibrant. Oh, and what have we here? Look at this little dainty."

Brie ambled over but didn't touch anything. I'm a toucher. I had the fabric between my fingers. This was lacy with sequins and glittery ribbons, all tan, white, and a touch of deep red.

"Ooh, this looks as though it barely covers the law, doesn't it?" I took it from the rack to hold it up in front of me and show Brie.

"Put that back! What are you doing, Vidalia? I don't think whoever has to wear that—"

"PUT THAT BACK!"

Before I could, the costume was snatched from my hands. A wiry, fast-moving fellow was replacing it on the rack. He had a light sheen of sweat on his face and arms. I stepped back.

"I am very sorry. I didn't mean to offend. I just admired the fabrics and colors."

The young man brushed himself down, as if wiping dust or dander from himself. He looked at me, finally. "You have no right touching the costumes. They're very expensive, you know." He was breathing rather hard for someone who looked to be in perfect shape and condition.

"Again, I'm sorry." I took a breath. "These costumes mean a lot to you, don't they? Are any of them for you? My name is Vidalia, and I just arrived here."

"I'm Dru. A couple of the shirts are mine. But this one you had in your hands is Isabelle's and it is extremely special, especially tonight. You scared me when I saw you handling it. Please, just move on." Dru dropped his hands to his sides and lowered his head, taking deep breaths.

We moved on.

"That was a little over the top, don't you think?" Brie asked as she took my elbow and guided me toward the patio.

"Maybe the costumes should have a guard or be put somewhere instead of the middle of the lobby if they're so valuable." I turned my head to look back at the costume rack. Dru was checking Isabelle's lacy costume.

"Gosh, it's not as though I put it on and went swimming in it. That guy is going all over the inside and outside of that costume. My hands are clean. He's the one sweating onto it. Let's get that cold drink."

Olive and Coco were sprawled in chairs on the outer edge of the patio with an unobstructed view of the water. Olive's bare feet were covered with sand.

"You didn't waste any time walking the beach, did you?" I asked.

"No, not one second," Olive responded. "I didn't have to go far or for long, but I had to feel the warm sand between my toes. I ground my heels into it. I feel anchored."

"What took you two so long?" Olive asked. "We've already ordered drinks. I asked for a rum punch without the rum."

"I would expect nothing less of you," I said.

"We unpacked and checked out the balcony for a few minutes," Brie said as she sat down.

"Of course you did," laughed Olive. "I'll bet your clothes are hung and your unmentionables are tucked into the drawers. I can picture your toiletries already lined up on the bathroom counter."

I wasn't going to bite at her attempt at sarcastic humor, no matter how accurate she was. I tossed my head back, caught her gaze on the way back to center, and with an even tone said, "Where else would they be?"

"I can't believe we're from the same family," Olive chuckled. "I opened my suitcase, pulled out this T-shirt and these shorts because they were on top, and dropped my travel clothes on the empty lid of the suitcase before we came down here." She waved her arm to our surroundings. "I can feel the dry skin sloughing off my feet already."

"Attractive thought," I snarked. "Thank you for sharing."

Brie looked at Coco. They both shook their heads. I sat down.

"Brie grew up with her French-Canadian grandmother who preached cleanliness is next to godliness, so she has neatness in her DNA. She's naturally neat and tidy." I smiled at Brie, who smiled sheepishly.

"I, however, grew up with a sign over our kitchen sink that said 'My house is clean enough to be healthy but dirty enough to be happy.' And that sums up much of the difference between Brie and me."

I tilted my head to one side and reflected on how I had become the way I am.

A waitress delivered a rum punch to me and one to Brie. We hadn't ordered them. Coco gave me a thumbs-up and gestured for me to continue.

"I think the neatness is also a survival skill. When I was a special education director with fifteen things going on at the same time, I used book bags to hold materials for each project or committee I was working on. Even if papers weren't filed exactly in the right place, they were at least in the right bag, so I could grab and go, knowing I had what I needed." I laughed at myself. "I called myself the bag lady of special education."

The memory of the bottom shelf of a bookcase in my office filled with book bags made me smile. It was a wonder I kept it together.

"Now," I continued, "my desk at home has piles according to project: writing, restaurant business, Mom's personal business, and church. Of course, any one of those piles could avalanche with the slightest tremor, but it works, mostly."

I took a breath and noticed raspberry-colored table linens and hollowed coconut vases with flowers as centerpieces going onto the tables around us. Technicians set up the sound system while others placed and checked the spotlights.

Brie came into my sweep of the area and she was giving me her "I know better" look.

"Okay," I admitted, "so maybe those contents scatter across piles and every so often I take over the kitchen counter to sort everything. I didn't say it was a foolproof strategy."

I looked out over the water. The sun was hovering above the horizon. A cruise ship was heading out from a day anchored in Phillipsburg and was the only thing that interrupted the seafoam-green ocean and near cloudless sky.

"It has been a long day of travel, and this rum punch is perfect. The air is perfect. It's February and I'm wearing a T-shirt and shorts. This is life, girls. Cheers to us," I declared. Coco chimed in, "Amen to that." She anchored one elbow on the table and leaned forward toward us. I knew we were in for a good story.

"It took me three days to get here. So I've actually been on vacation for half a week. This is just my next phase." She sat back and took a deep breath and blew it out with a low whistle.

"I left Anchorage and flew the red-eye to Denver. From there I went to Houston and had almost twenty-four hours of a layover."

Brie and I groaned. "What did you do?" I asked. "We would have gotten a hotel room and slept."

She grinned a Mona Lisa smirk. "I went out to a honky-tonk filled with cowboys and cowgirls and ate some barbecue." She bent her arms and swung her elbows side to side. "I wanted to keep up with the change in time zones so I kept moving."

"Did you scoot your boots while boogying in the line dancing?" Olive asked.

"Oh yes, I danced and twirled and stomped my feet. It was a gas." Coco threw her hands up in the air. "So, the next day I flew to San Juan. I was so close I could almost taste it but had another nineteen-hour opportunity for fun."

At this point, she pulled her phone out to show us pictures.

"This is Juan, my taxi driver and personal guide. He gave me a quick tour of Old San Juan. I almost broke my neck snapping it around to see each building he pointed out as we sped by. Then he took me to one of the fancy hotels." Coco raised her eyebrows as if impressed.

"We walked into the lobby of this glittery, colorful, somewhat dated hotel, with me on his arm as if he owned the place. He was greeted by the maître d' and they chatted in some language I didn't understand, but we all smiled at one another."

"Did you think for an instant that you might never see your home or family again during any of this?" Brie asked.

"Nope. Juan waved and left, tapping his watch."

"What? He just left you there?" Olive's voice was a little higher in pitch.

"Sure. So, I sat at the bar and listened to the live music for a couple of hours. There were a couple of professional dancers who flew over that dance floor." She shook her head in disbelief. "I caught enough to learn they were practicing for a competition and the hotel let them use the space and music if they called it entertainment. It was cool. I donated a little bit to their tip jar. Those costumes don't come cheap."

I just gawked at her. "Never ever would I have the courage to do that. So then what happened?"

"Juan came back for me in time for my flight. I'll tell you, by then, I was in my Caribbean state of mind. Hopscotching from San Juan to here was a blip on the screen. I got here so relaxed and happy I was vibrating at a whole other frequency. Still am."

"And you haven't even started your conference yet," Brie said.

Coco slapped her palm onto the table, making our drinks jump and wobble.

"I know, right? I cannot wait to hear about how they handled infectious diseases here." She caught the looks from people nearby and lowered her voice considerably. "Maybe I'll talk about that when we're away from dining areas."

"Nothing gets by you," Olive said.

Chapter Five

All of a sudden, a small whooshing sound a few feet from our table caught our attention and a tiki torch flamed to life. The dozen or so torches surrounding the patio flared up. Party lights over the bar came on, and twinkling lights filled in the spaces with happy light. Fire pits on the adjoining beach silhouetted the palm trees. A festive atmosphere grew as guests took their seats.

Yes, dear reader, we had sat through the entire setup, taking up one of the tables. We had been oblivious to the fact that our table was included in the very patio that staff had been transforming. Two seasoned staff members recognized our exhaustion-induced dull-headedness; they cleared our table and started to reset it. Their coordinated movements showed us that we weren't their first table of airheads.

"Oh! We're sorry!" we all said, standing up and pushing our chairs away from the table and out of the way.

"No matter, ladies," the taller staff member said.

I started to help place the tablecloth, and both staff stopped moving.

"Perhaps madame might help," said the taller one while handing me the napkins. I had intruded on their routine.

Coco said, "Just let the nice people do their jobs, Vidalia. We've done enough."

The staff looked at Coco, nodded, and smiled before resuming their work.

We resettled into our now-festive table complete with flowers in a coconut shell. A reggae band in fruit bowl colored shirts and black slacks played steel drums and sang. Rum punch and wine were served.

Olive asked for decaf iced tea, and it was delivered with an umbrella and cherry/pineapple garnish. She cooed. I clapped with glee. We'd already gotten our money's worth.

"We are not the most underdressed for this event," I breathed a small sigh of relief.

"But we certainly have been eclipsed by some of the more festive guests," Brie commented.

"Travel has changed, hasn't it?" Coco asked.

"True, we see baggy jeans and T-shirts at every kind of event nowadays. People don't dress up anymore. No more dressing to impress. It's all about comfort," I said.

"Not everyone got that memo because some of these people are dressed to the nines," Olive observed. "Some of the sundresses are beautiful. The jewelry looks like family jewels, you know? Look at that woman's pearl necklace and matching earrings. She touches them lightly, like she's bringing the family or the love with her. I'll bet she and her husband are celebrating an anniversary."

"Yes," I chimed in. "I bet they're from Chicago and he bought her those pearls and earrings after he won his first law case. It was their first achievement together as a couple."

"All those years ago," Olive continued the thread. "Look at them smiling at each other and the care he is taking to seat her and order their drinks." She rubbed her palms together, energizing the story line.

"And they're off," Brie said. "Coco, does Olive do this when she's visiting you in Alaska? Does she see people and fabricate entire stories about them?"

Coco laughed. "Sometimes Olive will create a line or two to get us started, but—"

Olive interrupted her. "Coco usually adds something over-the-top for my refined tastes. I start nervous laughing, which spurs her raucous laughter. The very people we're making up a story about start looking at us so I have to shut us down. That Coco is a wild one. She's Hot Coco."

"With a dash of red chili pepper for spice," Coco added with what could only be described as a Cheshire-cat grin.

Our storytelling ended when a microphone squealed. People covered their ears and hollered. We laughed and applauded when it ended. Mr. Maricopa introduced himself as the resort manager. He wore white slacks and an untucked tan shirt that brought out his shiny chestnut-brown hair and long eyelashes. Even from across the patio, his green eyes were full of merriment and life. He wasn't a tall man, rather rectangular built, trim but not buff.

"Eeyow!" he yelled, holding the microphone at arm's length with his right hand and covering his left ear with the other. He laughed and shook his head back and forth.

"Good evening, ladies and gentlemen. Sorry for that opening racket, but I can promise you that it will be the worst sound you hear tonight. My name is Francis Maricopa, and I am manager here at Peacock Beach Resort. Welcome to this slice of paradise. We are pleased to have you with us, especially tonight, as we enjoy the songs and dances of our island and beyond." He tugged the front hem of his shirt down and smoothed the fabric across his chest.

"Tonight, we have our own island songbird, Isabelle Simone. She has been on tour and is back specifically for this very special fundraising event for our orphanage, which sustained severe fire damage in the Records Room. Many original documents were destroyed, and these were the only personal history our children had."

He nodded his head, acknowledging the sad impact his story was having on the audience.

"It is very sad, my friends. Birth records, church and family records will not be available to the children when they reach maturity. Their only hope for learning about their birth families has gone up in smoke." Mr. Maricopa raised his hand upward to the open sky.

"So tonight we build again. Money raised this evening will first," he held up one finger, "repair the damage from the fire to restore the beautiful building to its original appearance. But more than that, your generosity will…" He took a piece of paper from his pocket and read, "Secure the technology needed to have all records saved digitally off-site, safe from any chance of destruction." He nodded with a smile, stuffing the paper back into his pocket.

"Yes, you saw that I read those words, 'saved digitally thus and so.' I do not understand what that means, but I know enough to feel relief that records will become more than simple pieces of paper that can burn. Tonight is not for sadness but for hope and moving forward.

As I said, Isabelle Simone is here to sing and dance her way into your pockets. Wait."

He turned his head to the side and paused. "That didn't come out right." He smiled wide. "Then again, maybe it did." He shrugged. There were a few chuckles from the crowd.

"Isabelle has been a lifelong benefactor of the Saint Gerolamo Emiliani Orphanage. As a schoolgirl, she would perform with friends in fundraisers for the orphanage. She danced with the children and took some of them under her wing. You will be introduced to some of those lucky ones tonight." There were warm murmurs from some of the women.

"He's greasing up those wallets, isn't he?" I said softly.

Brie responded, "Oh yeah, this guy has his patter and ramp-up down to a science. I've seen women patting their husbands' thighs near their wallets to get them ready. The lady at the next table asked the waitress if personal checks were accepted."

"Tssst," Olive chastised us. "Let the man do his job and let these wealthy people give what they can. You two are party poopers."

"This isn't our first fundraiser. We are merely appreciating a fine job when we hear and see it," I flipped back at my sister. "These things just don't happen, you know. Everyone has their role."

Mr. Maricopa raised his voice and waved the crowd toward him. "Welcome, welcome, one and all to this night of song and dance and much, much more! Are you ready for some fun?" Applause erupted. "Please give a warm welcome to our emcee for tonight, another island favorite, Bertrand D'Lamore!"

A tall, thin man with close-cropped curly black hair; a long, straight nose; and eyes the color of warm brown velvet came in. He held a microphone in his left hand, shook hands and gave a half-hug to Mr. Maricopa.

"Thank you, Francis. Thank you, ladies and gentlemen." He bowed, smiled, waved, and bowed again. He nodded to the band and music started.

"We come from many places, but we are all welcome." He began to sing "Willkommen" from *Cabaret*. Some of us recognized the tune and nodded assent. Toes started tapping under some tables. My shoulders were already shifting and swaying to the beat.

With the steel drums and horns backing him up, his sexy expressions and dance moves, he set the mood. Perhaps some straight women were also feeling invited to something more, but we all felt welcomed.

He finished the song with the band pushing the limits of their instruments, and the energy in the patio was high and going higher. Applause was loud and fast.

"Thank you, ladies and gentlemen. We bring you our own flavor of cabaret with a variety of performers to entertain you. I am Bertrand D'Lamore, and I will be your emcee for this evening. I myself grew up on Saint Martin. I work as a water engineer at the desalination plant. You may thank me for the delicious water on your tables, eh? How do we get all of that salt out of the water for its many uses?" He chuckled. "That is a story for another time. Tonight, I have polished my dancing shoes and warmed up my voice as I did during my school days in order to support tonight's worthy efforts." Bertrand danced a little time step and gave a bow.

"While you enjoy your dinner, the band will keep your toes tapping and spirits high. The show will begin just as dessert is being served. Enjoy." He walked off the patio, and wait staff served our first course.

A small bowl of chilled black bean and mango soup was set before each of us. White bowls with a small curled lip, like a tulip, held the thin broth melding all of the chopped ingredients together. The black beans and bright orange-yellow mango popped with the yellow and orange bell peppers, carrots, and string beans. A feast for my eyes.

"This is so happening at the Grand," Olive oozed. "Usually I blend the black beans until smooth, but these soft and crunchy textures are fun."

"And this dollop of crème fraiche blends it all beautifully." Brie smacked her lips.

"We could offer a choice of sour cream or soy cheese and make everyone's mouth happy." Olive kept creating.

Coco added, "A few chunks of kielbasa wouldn't hurt."

Brie gave her a silent thumbs-up as Olive ignored that suggestion completely.

As we finished the first course, Olive sighed and pushed her bowl away. "My purpose here is done. I've been here less than a day and I've already found a soup recipe. This is so good." She licked her spoon.

Between each course came a thin spear of fresh pineapple to cleanse the palate.

Our entrée was a fresh, local whitefish with salad. This was not just any whitefish, my friend. It was cod, jeweled with colorful bell peppers, diced pimentos, chopped parsley, and tomatoes.

"This is a party for my eyes," I said. "Talk about eating the rainbow. How did they get the fish for this many people to remain flaky and not mushy? It's great."

I dabbed my mouth with my napkin. "Brie and I have small wishes for this week, and I'm wondering what yours are." I looked from my sister to her friend.

One of them gave me a deadpan expression. Guess who?

I started us off. "Well, for myself, I want to swim in the ocean every single day."

Fortunately, Coco was willing to play along.

"I hope to attend every session of the medical conference, but I know myself too well and expect to do something fun every day I'm here." She grinned. "When I get back from Saba each day, I'm hoping you three will still have energy enough to go someplace terrific for dinner and see what else might avail itself to us. A salsa band or flamenco dancers. Food and fun, those are my wants. Now what about you, Olive? What have you reflected about and sincerely wish to have happen while you're here?" She jabbed Olive in the ribs with a big smile.

"What?" Olive's face was all scrunched up in confusion and bewilderment. "Oh yes, I sat for hours—hours, I tell you—contemplating how to make the most of this experience physically and spiritually. Oh yeah, that's me, the planner." She shook her head. "You guys make my head hurt." She took a swallow of her iced tea and rolled her eyes as she set the tumbler down. "I can feel myself tightening up just thinking about planning. Why don't we just get up every day and decide what we want to do?"

"Okay, slow down, sissa," I chuckled. "Maybe you can be delighted each day when we present you with our plans because some experiences require advance tickets or reservations. Since you're open to just about anything, leave the planning to us."

Gosh, that ice-cold chardonnay was good. I put my dinner fork across my plate.

"Brie wants to take a good walk on the beach each day. You can join either of us if you want."

"Sounds like a great plan." She elbowed Coco and nodded her head.

Our salads started with a bed of shredded lettuce. Over that was a mixture of diced tomato, cucumber, celery, and shredded carrots. On top of all that was a layer of almost slivered avocado.

"How'd they get this avocado so thin?" Coco lifted up a piece with her knife.

We all examined our avocado. I looked around, and yes, we were the only ones.

"It's not as though you can slap an avocado onto a mandoline or cheese slicer," I lifted up part of mine with my fork.

Brie and Olive said at the same time, "Uh-oh, another new kitchen gadget!"

Olive looked around. "I'll ask what they use in the kitchen later."

"Probably a very calm person with a steady hand and a very sharp knife," Brie mused.

The vinaigrette dressing had white wine vinegar, Dijon mustard, crushed garlic, pepper, salt, and a touch of olive oil. "This dressing would make a great bread dip. I could drink this stuff by the spoonful." Olive pushed her lettuce around to get more dressing.

Dessert, which I had saved room for, was thinly sliced plantain rounds, fried like potato chips and dusted with cinnamon sugar. There was just a drizzle of melted dark chocolate that perfected it.

"The crunch! The salty and sweet—scrumptious!" I used my finger to lap up chocolate from my plate and licked it off my finger. "This chocolate is just right. I'm a happy woman."

Chapter Six

As we finished eating, Bertrand D'Lamore walked onto the patio holding the hand of the first child in a line of about a dozen youngsters. They looked to range in age from six to sixteen. They were all whistling "You Are My Sunshine." A young woman brought up the end of the line.

"He looks like a proud uncle, doesn't he?" Olive whispered.

All table conversations stopped. Each of the young people wore navy-blue Bermuda shorts and sandals. Their T-shirts were either aqua blue or cantaloupe orange, with what must have been the St. Emiliani Home logo where a pocket would have been.

Bertrand helped get the kids into a semicircle while the woman got their attention and kept it. Bertrand walked to the side of the stage.

She said a few things to them that we couldn't hear. Busy hands became still at their sides. The woman blew into a pitch pipe and her arms came up. Every eye was on her, including my own. I knew authority when I saw it.

Without introduction, they began to sing in French. I looked over to trilingual Brie.

"I recognize it but can't remember the name," she said.

"Don't bother trying to interpret for us, just let yourself enjoy it," I patted her thigh.

After brief applause, the children went right into "This Little Light of Mine" in English. The tiniest of the children couldn't have been more endearing. The preteens looked hopeful, and the teens looked determined.

"Can you see the resiliency in their eyes? Some of the older kids look as though this is a theme song for them. No one is going to blow out their light. That's good to see," Olive said softly.

The song ended, and our applause was warm and full.

The woman took a microphone from Bertrand and started to speak. We couldn't hear her. The mic wasn't on. She threw a look over to Bertrand, who suppressed a giggle. She turned the microphone on and started again.

"Oh that Bertrand, always playing with me." She smiled a coquettish grin at him and then looked our way and winked. "I don't mind. We have known one another all of our lives." She stood straighter and shook her head.

"Enough silliness. Ladies and gentleman, thank you for your warm reception of our children of St. Emiliani's. My name is Donna Fleur, and I am their song and dance coach." She took a moment, much like a teacher waiting for all eyes to be on her.

"I myself am an orphan. I was raised by the family of caregivers at this very same orphanage." She glanced off to the side while her hand went to her chest. She patted it twice before continuing. "It is the home of the only family I have ever known." She looked down at the floor and swallowed.

Her head popped up, she stood tall with a broad smile and said, 'I turned out all right, don't you agree?'

Cheers and applause seemed to fortify her. She looked at the youngsters. "You will turn out just fine, too, sisters and brothers. I won't leave you behind like—"

She stopped herself and turned back to us.

"When I grew too old to remain at the orphanage, I began working full-time with tonight's headliner, Isabelle Simone. We have danced and sung together since grade school. Now we perform on all the islands. It is very exciting. When we return to Saint Martin, I go back to my home, like any loyal family member, and teach these young ones what others have taught me. Music and dance let me escape my young fears and doubts."

I could only imagine what doubts and fears go through an orphan's mind.

"Dancing and singing raised me up," she continued. "I could see that there could be more to my life than what I knew. It saved me." She took a breath. "We will close with our theme song, 'Spirit of Life.'"

Donna handed the microphone to one of the older boys, a tall, lanky teenager.

"My name is Jordan." He flicked his thick, wavy black hair out of his eyes with a head toss. "I am fifteen years old. My goal is to become an engineer, like Bertrand." His eyes flitted over toward Bertrand. "I want to bring clean drinking water to people who need it."

There was loud applause, and a few 'Atta boys!'" shouted.

He continued. "Saint Martin is a land of many spiritual beliefs. Whether it is God, Buddha, or Mother Nature herself. This song is our prayer."

He handed the microphone to Bertrand, who accepted it and shook the young man's hand.

"Spirit of Life, come unto me." The singers held their hands open to the sky.

"Sing in my heart, all the stirrings of compassion." They put both hands to their hearts.

"Blow in the wind." They waved their fingers across the front of their chests.

"Rise in the sea." Their hands made wave motions.

"Move in the hand, giving life the shape of justice." They opened their hands again, then put thumb to forefinger and moved their hands up and down like the scales of justice.

"Roots hold me close." They took one another's hands.

"Wings set me free." Their hands broke apart and fluttered skyward.

"Spirit of Life, come to me." Their hands came down, resting on their hearts.

"Come to me."

Not a sound. Only breathing.

Then came the applause with shouts of "Amen!" and "Alleluia!"

One woman said, "I want a copy of that song."

Another asked, "Do you think they have a recording we can buy?"

The youngsters smiled wide, bowed, and began walking off the patio.

As Bertrand came from the edge of the patio, he reached for Donna's hand as she walked by. He stopped her and kissed her hand. She looked pleased with the acknowledgment.

"Aren't these young people great?" he asked, turning to us. "They are my heroes." He watched them leave. "Now they will have a dinner here at the resort, maybe use the pool before heading home. Your support tonight helps lift those children. Thank you."

Everyone was smiling.

"And now for a more adult version of tonight's festivities." Bertrand sang a coquettish love song in French. Brie minimally translated and Olive, Coco, and I changed the words so the story wasn't stereotypically man-dominated. Our giggles were a bit too loud and slightly out of place, if the expressions of guests at nearby tables bore any merit. That made the three of us titter even more, and Brie pretended she didn't know us.

Bertrand described island lore while shirtless, dark-skinned men in shorts appeared and scaled the nearby palm trees or began dancing on the patio. Bertrand dramatically brought us through the dangers, hunt, deprivation, and final victory of the aboriginal group of the island. The finale had women in voluminous skirts and tight bodices dancing and singing with the men. The women's strapless dresses were in shades of candy-apple red, saffron gold, tangerine orange, Granny-Smith-apple green, and aqua blue. Bertrand took the lead vocal and the hand of the most voluptuous female dancer, Donna.

"Oh!" I said. "There she is again."

She seemed to glow when she was dancing with Bertrand. They all twirled, swirled, bobbed, wove, and jumped to the climactic end, and everyone was on their feet clapping and cheering.

Bertrand mopped his brow, shook off the heat from his shirtsleeves, and got a serious face on. His voice was lower now, and we leaned forward with anticipation.

"Ladies and gentlemen, it is time to bring you the big fish from our little island. The woman who has become so successful she has to travel the world to contain her spirit, beauty, and lyrical voice. Bella—" He stopped and looked up. "Oops, oh my, I apologize," he said. "That is what I called Miss Simone in our younger years together. You see,

I know this lady." Bertrand snickered and looked at the crowd with a devilish eye. "Oh yes, I could tell you things!"

He wiped his brow with his handkerchief dramatically, winking at the crowd, pausing for dramatic effect. He pulled his composure back to the emcee he was hired to be that evening and continued.

"But nothing I tell you could diminish the voice and beauty of this remarkable woman. She and her musicians grace us with their presence tonight to sing and dance for us in hopes that we will open our hearts and pocketbooks to provide essential care to the wonderful, bright, and funny children in the Saint Emiliani Home for Children. Ladies and gentlemen, please welcome Isabelle Simone."

Isabelle Simone strutted into the area with a loud music-backed entrance. She strutted in those stiletto heels with ankle straps like they were flip flops. A last adjustment to her headset microphone and she was ready to perform. She gave Bertrand a polite, customary hug and cheek-kiss. Bertrand's expression melted. He took Isabelle into his arms for a full-body hug. His chin rested on the top of her head. He closed his eyes. Then he whispered something into her ear and walked away.

Isabelle stepped back, made a dance-like spin so her back was to the audience for a second. Her head was down, and she had her arms around her waist. A split second later, she whirled around to us and the drummer counted off the beat.

I leaned over to Olive. "Did you see that body language? He was gyrating and full of sex two seconds ago. Then he looks like, I don't know, like what?"

"Yeah," she said, "Those two aren't just friends, is my guess. I'll bet she could tell stories about him, too."

"Maybe their story isn't over," Coco said.

Isabelle sang a come-hither song. Brie and Coco were in fiesta delight, arms akimbo and making wavelike moves. We clapped along and butt-danced in our chairs. No one could sit still. Isabelle slithered, ground her hips, and spun into a high-volume, full twerking climax. Understanding French wasn't necessary to interpret the meaning of the song, and many of the men were happier than their wives would have liked them to be.

"Ladies and gentlemen, thank you for your warm welcome to me and my bandmates." She took a little side step and put one hand to her head. "Ooh! Can you get jet lag flying between islands? I didn't think so, but something has my head aflutter. I'll have to check with my manager and friend Stefan Dolares. Stefan, please stand and be recognized. This is the man who arranges not just our performances but travel, hotels, and eating. He is amazing. Thank you, Stefan."

A light-skinned man wearing khakis and a golf shirt stood and waved.

Isabelle straightened up. "When we heard about this event for our children of St. Emiliani, we could not stay away. We resolved to put away other plans to be here with you this evening. Our most vulnerable brothers and sisters need our help. Remember," and she began singing, "Greatest Love of All." Reminding us to teach children to have pride in themselves and to cling to their dignity no matter what others say or do. It was powerful.

I was singing and weeping from my seat right along with Isabelle.

She looked over at Bertrand. He was singing along, too. There wasn't a dry eye in the place. Men patted their wives' knees. Women patted their noses.

"Thank you, ladies and gentlemen," Isabelle continued. "Just before I came out here, Monsieur Michel Tipo from the orphanage informed me that from your generous ticket purchases alone, we have raised two thousand eight hundred dollars for the children of the orphanage. Bless you."

After some applause, she cocked one hand on her hip and took a quick look around. "If you know me, you know that I don't," she slid her hand down her thigh, then back up and across her flat stomach, "how shall I say it, with a final swath up between her breasts, satisfy easily." She brought her hand back down to her hip.

"Two thousand eight hundred dollars is a respectable sum. But I'm not satisfied. So? I won't leave this stage tonight until Monsieur Michel tells me we have collected four thousand dollars.

How will I do it, you ask?" Isabelle looked her body up and down. "Oh, what do I have that others may want?" Her eyes slid over to some of the husbands. "I will start by auctioning off my necklace." Isabelle's eyes went to a woman in the front and gave her a nod. Women started beaming.

"Bertrand, will you help me, please?"

He strode across to her and put his hands on her shoulders. Standing behind Isabelle, he unhooked the gold-glittered choker necklace with a fringe of strung gold and clear beads hanging down onto her chest. One end slipped out of his hand and fell onto her chest, dancing lightly on her breast. With gentle care, his pinky finger latched onto the stray end and swept it up. They just gazed at each other.

They broke into a chuckle as he handed Isabelle the jewelry. She held it up for all to see, strutting around the patio for women and smart husbands to take a closer look. People began shouting out numbers of US dollars they would pay for it. Isabelle wrangled that microphone like an old-time auctioneer and got a couple to bid three hundred dollars. She collected the cash from the husband and slid it into her bosom, connected the necklace around the wife's neck, and kissed them both on the cheek.

"I don't know what else I may have to take off this evening to sell for these children, but my pledge remains. I will stay here until we reach four thousand dollars."

The crowd went wild.

Isabelle called for different dancers from backstage who came out, full of fun and spirit. Audience members bid against one another for the opportunity to dance with backup dancers as Isabelle sang. Women from the American Midwest paid to dance with exotic island men while Isabelle sang about their deepest desires. The male dancers did their part by looking longingly at the women and dancing suggestively. At the end of every song, cash was handed to Isabelle that she would slip into her sequined and jewel-studded bra.

"I'm getting me some of this!" Coco bid and won. The muscular dancer was shirtless, and his slacks looked painted on.

"My name is Dru, and it will be my pleasure to dance with you."

"Yes, it will, you little bit of wonderful," Coco responded, already swaying.

A bandana around his neck came off, and he used it to go around Coco's neck and down her backside, pulling her closer all the time. "Woo-hoo!" she yelled. He looked pleasantly surprised. Coco's body had become gelatinous. They both had a good time. The palm trees on her blouse were a-shimmying and a-shakin'. He went down on his knees and back up again with less than a breath between them. Her head was up one beat and down the next. Her hair was flipping in every direction, a red flame.

I was up and taking pictures and video with my camera. No one would believe this sight. Olive had one hand over her eyes, but she was peeking through her fingers, shaking her head.

Brie's smile could not have been wider. "That one kills me."

Coco came back to the table one hot, sweaty mess. Limp as a rag doll. With a loud chortle, she smacked her hand on the table. "Now that's what I'm talkin' about. I'm going to love this place. I can just feel it."

Coco's dancer brought the cash for his dance to Isabelle.

"Oh, Dru, my good friend." She adjusted her headset. "It isn't just me who enjoys a good romp with you, is it?" He had a huge grin. Instead of handing the money to her, Dru slipped it into Isabelle's bra.

"Oh! Oh my. He's a little comfortable with her breasts, wouldn't you say?" Olive squirmed.

Isabelle winced and grabbed at his hand, covering it. His hand lingered, with the placement of those bills, between her breast and the costume. They shared a look. His was more than friendly. Hers was a warning glance. When he lowered his head to kiss and make it all better, she slapped him and he staggered a couple of feet away. The men in the audience felt his pain. "You lose, buddy."

"I would have knocked him into next week," Olive sneered.

Isabelle seemed to stagger to one of the front tables and rested her fingertips on it. She took a sip of water from one of the glasses on the table without asking. As she set the glass down, she looked at one of the women and said, "Excuse me and thank you."

Isabelle took a couple steps back onto the dance floor.

"Oh my friends, who will pay for me? Everyone else has danced while I sang. Now, I feel like dancing. How much am I worth?"

Bidding was high for a chance to dance with Isabelle. The crowd was surprised when the winner, Bertrand D'Lamore, walked onto the patio with a fistful of cash raised high. Isabelle's eyes went wide. Bertrand handed her the cash, never taking his eyes off hers, and Isabelle slid the cash into her bosom. He took Isabelle's hand while placing his other hand low on her hip. He nodded to the band. He had a head mic on, too.

"Do you think that was planned?" I asked.

The music started, Bertrand took the lead on the dance, and Isabelle sputtered to hit her first notes. She faltered and Bertrand sang low and smoothly to support her. He had an "I'm not going anywhere, babe" look in his eyes, and Isabelle struggled to keep singing. The power had shifted on stage; now Bertrand had it. Isabelle's face looked confused. She swung her head around to look at all of us.

She gave a little head shake, played the crowd with a dramatic swoon that almost looked like she was fainting. Bertrand's strong hand brought her back up against him. They swayed rhythmically together, ending in a full-body kiss. There was a musical crescendo that came to a full stop while the two continued to kiss. It was magic. Pictures and video were taken. People kissed each other. Ooh, it was simply magic.

As the two separated, Isabelle dropped to the floor.

Chapter Seven

Uh-oh, that must have hurt.

Bertrand D'Lamore sat on the patio floor cradling a limp Isabelle Simone in his arms.

"*Bon ange, bon ange.* Stay here with me." His head microphone was still on. Bertrand removed a necklace from under his shirt and placed it around Isabelle's neck. It was a rawhide cord with a coal-black figurine hanging from it.

"Don't be afraid. This will help you."

I felt like I was watching an intimate scene that I'd just happened upon. He didn't seem to be aware that any of us were still there.

There was no curtain to pull to give them privacy. Managers, crew, and backup performers were crowding into the small area. Someone called for emergency medical help.

"What is happening?" I looked to Coco. Coco was already assessing what had become a medical event.

Mr. Maricopa came out and took charge. He clapped his hands twice and everyone stopped talking and yelling.

"Secure, evacuate, report." Staff began moving in a methodical manner.

Some went to the perimeter of the area, pulling out their cell phones as they moved. A few were already taking pictures and video. I could tell because they were scanning the crowd. Other staff escorted guests away from the area, typing their names into their cell phones.

A waiter took a couple from the next table. "If you'll come with me, please. What is your name? Yes, Mr. and Mrs. Buzzell." He typed in the names. "In which apartment? Yes, thank you, number 412." He looked back at his phone and typed quickly.

"If you'll come with me, I will escort you back into the lobby so you may return to your rooms." He put one arm around the back of Mr. Buzzell, not touching him, but herding him and his wife.

"We are asking all guests to remain in the resort until your account of what happened can be taken. Thank you in advance for your understanding and cooperation." As soon as the Buzzells were at the lobby door, he swung around and went after another couple.

From chaos to calm with three words. Impressive.

"This is amazing! They must have emergency procedures that they actually adhere to," I observed.

Coco was on her feet scanning for someone with higher medical authority than she had, someone to take the lead. Olive, Brie, and I sat very still.

Far up the beach, there was an animal screech of some kind. It sounded ghastly. A few employees looked toward the sound, and their faces took on a look of recognition. They closed their eyes momentarily and when they opened them, their eyes held a resolution, a somber acceptance. They each looked at Isabelle with a compassionate nod of their head. People gathered in small groups on the beach. Those who had heard and understood the significance of the animal screech were explaining something to others. Brie got up and joined one of those groups.

The head waiter handed tablecloths to staff to obscure the view of the looky-loos. I noticed Donna, dance teacher and backup for Isabelle, holding one of the table linens. Her face was expressionless. She didn't cry or try to be with Isabelle. Probably in shock, poor thing. Coco was assisting a doctor from the audience, who was examining Isabelle, allowing Bertrand to keep Isabelle in his arms. Just as the tablecloths were about to cut off our view, Coco tossed Olive a look.

Olive interpreted it in a whisper, "Oh crap, she's dead. We should go. Coco will catch up with us when she's done."

An emergency medical team wheeled in a gurney while the doctor continued his examination. Olive and I left our table, cautious not to scuff our chairs on the patio floor. We didn't want to interrupt or intrude. A staffer took our names and apartment numbers. We walked into the airy lobby and sank into one of the sofas. Brie joined us.

"Did we just watch a woman die?" I knew the answer but was struggling to absorb it all.

Olive kept the questions coming. "How does someone just die like that? She didn't grab her chest for a heart attack or show any of the signs of a stroke. How does that just happen?" Her hands went up in despair.

"The autopsy will reveal all of the answers, if the two of you can be patient." Brie looked at us through half-lidded eyes.

"Before you fall asleep, Brie, did you find out what that awful animal sound was?" I rubbed her arm.

"Yes, quite interesting, actually. One of the religious groups believes that when an animal perishes at the same time as a human, the two spirits join forces, so to speak, making their way into paradise easier. One complements the other. The people I listened to already know that Isabelle has left her body."

"Yes, but that chicken, or whatever it was, didn't die a natural death. It sounded like it was being strangled." I rubbed my neck.

"Yes, another interesting point." Brie looked back out onto the patio area. "If a religious prophet or seer senses someone will die and may need help moving to the other side, that seer will sacrifice an animal."

She started in again on that iPad. "Isabelle is from Saint Martin, so the body won't have to be transferred across international boundaries. That's a relief for whoever has to make decisions."

Olive and I just looked at Brie. We knew this was how she worked—on facts. Nothing at all like how we operated. We usually looked for the drama, the story.

Over by the registration desk, Mr. Tipo, head of the orphanage, was talking with Mr. Maricopa, a uniformed police officer, and two other men in suits. Olive and I watched them. Mr. Tipo was shifting from foot to foot, arms clamped across his chest, almost protectively. The officer was standing tall, leaning into the conversation with an eye-lock on Mr. Tipo.

The officer removed a clear plastic evidence bag from his inside jacket pocket, opened it, and leaned closer to Mr. Tipo, whose face was crestfallen with a tinge of rage. He took a bundle of cash out of his jacket and placed it into the bag. Before he let go, Mr. Tipo pulled out a marker and wrote on the bag "$4,000.00 USD for St. Emiliani Orphanage." Then he wrote "$4,000.00 USD" on his own hand. He held his hand in a stop-like position, in the officer's face, said something about the bag of money, turned and walked out of the lobby. The officer and resort manager resumed talking.

"Well, that was interesting." Olive swept a strand of hair behind her ear. "Maybe Mr. Tipo is worried he won't get all of his money returned. I can guess how easily cash might go missing."

From the patio/beach area, the EMT crew wheeled the gurney with Isabelle's body on it through the lobby. She was covered head to toe with a sheet.

"Oh crap, just like in the movies," I said. "When the sheet covers the face, the patient no longer needs fresh air."

Brie's eyes slid over to look at me with disbelief. "How do you think of these things? No longer needs fresh air?"

"Tell me what I said that isn't true?" I asked.

"Uh-oh, Coco's in the middle of the mix." Olive watched a group coming from the patio into the lobby. "Why am I not surprised?"

Coco moved along with the doctor and medical crew. She would stay with them as long as she could. She tossed us a look and a little wave that conveyed she was okay and eager to follow this opportunity. Jane Wayne, that's our Coco.

Bertrand D'Lamore walked through the lobby next, his head down and face somber. A female officer was escorting him. To his car? To the police station?

The crew and other performers came through carrying sound and lighting equipment. Stefan Dolares checked equipment and seemed to be supervising. They were all pretty quiet, speaking only to give orders about packing equipment. He repeated that he would stay connected with each of them as more was known and reminded them to go home and stay there until police interviewed each of them. Stefan was patting them on the shoulder while looking at his iPad. He was the manager, all right. He was managing this big family of performers and crew.

Dru, the male lead dancer who had danced with Coco, the same one who had yelled at me for touching costumes, and got slapped by

Isabelle, was on his phone texting the hell out of it to whoever he was sending it to. He was silently weeping. His shoulders, heaving and slumped forward, didn't look like those of a dancer. When that text was finished, he stood tall, flipped his shoulders back, and strode with purpose toward Stefan Dolares.

The female officer walked back into the lobby.

The manager put one arm around the dancer's shoulder and steered him toward the patio. Dru tried to wriggle his shoulders out of Stefan's grasp. The officer saw this and walked over. Dru's eyes went wide, and he struggled even more to be freed. The officer raised both hands to calm him down. Dru caught us watching.

"She was holding Isabelle's costume before the show! I caught her!" He was pointing a shaking finger right at me.

Now my eyes were wide. We all sat motionless and soundless on the sofa. I tried to breathe. The female officer looked at another officer and jerked her head toward us. He nodded and immediately headed our way.

"Ohmygod, ohmygod, ohmygod," I whisper-prayed as I watched him approach. I swear he was seven feet tall and probably former special ops.

"May I sit with you ladies?" (good start.)

"Yes, please." We each shifted to make room for this smooth, baritone-voiced man as he navigated our legs and the coffee table in front of us as if it were practiced choreography.

"My name is Officer Anton Williams assigned to take your statements of what you saw and heard during this evening's event." He looked at each of us. "And I will ask you, madam, what that fellow was talking about, but all in good time. Why don't we start with your names and where you're from?" He took out the obligatory flip notebook and clicked his pen.

We told him.

"Okay, that's good. Now please, one at a time, tell me what you saw and heard from the time you came onto the patio to the time Ms. Simone collapsed." He kept his head down, pen poised, and waited until one of us spoke first. I couldn't stand it.

"We had just arrived at the resort and were having a drink on the patio as it was being set up. So we—"

Officer Williams raised a hand to stop me. "Please tell me what you saw and heard. The others will tell me their perspectives and memories afterward. Go on." His head went back to his notepad.

I felt lost. How could I tell a story without Olive and Brie chiming in? Officer Williams looked back up at me with one eyebrow raised.

"Um, you see, we don't work like that. I am part of this threesome, and when one tells a story, the other two correct, add, and clarify. We're like pound puppies—all over each other."

He kept his brow raised and kept looking at me.

"But I can try, can't I, Officer? Yes, I can and I will. Okay, let's see." I told him every detail I could, and he probably wished he'd brought a stenographer with him.

After he shook his writing hand out after finishing his notes on me, Officer Williams asked Olive and Brie.

Olive was nervous of law enforcement and used a bulleted list.

"Pretty much what Vidalia said—we just got here; I walked a little of the beach before drinks. I, by the way, don't drink alcohol. People came in; the event started; we ate. Oh my good God, the food was sooooo good."

The officer raised his face and that eyebrow to my sister.

"Oh, okay, yes, I see. I'll get that soup recipe, though. Okay, back to what happened. The kids sang—so cute; Bertrand sang; Isabelle came out; dancing, singing, money being raised; she and Bertrand, I think they were in love—I'm just saying what I saw; and she collapsed. My friend Coco became part of the rescue and emergency team, and she left with them. She's a nurse."

"Thank you, Ms. Ahern. And now we come to you, madam." He turned to Brie, who had her iPad steaming, she had been typing so fast.

"Yes, Officer Williams. I have been typing up my report while you've been interviewing these two. I can read it to you or send it to you electronically—whichever is more efficient for you, sir."

(Did I tell you that I love this woman?)

The officer reached for the iPad and read the statement. Remember that Brie was a history major and worked for a congressman. Chronological reports of facts are one of her strengths.

"Ah, Ms. Quirion, I see that you have a keen attention to detail. If you would send this to me at this email address, I would appreciate it."

He handed Brie his card. She nodded and scooched over to send the email immediately.

He came back to me.

"Now, Ms. Ahern. Perhaps I'll refer to you as Ms. V. Ahern to distinguish the two sisters, eh? Ms. V. Ahern, would you tell me please what that fellow was shouting about?"

I closed my eyes and took a couple of breaths.

"Sure. Brie and I were walking through the lobby and I saw the rack of costumes. The colors and fabrics were bold and lovely, I went to have a closer look."

Officer Williams was writing and looked up at me when I stopped. I thought I was done.

"Ms. V. Ahern, what happened that he," pointing his thumb over his shoulder to indicate Dru, "said that he caught you?"

"Oh, that. Well, the costumes were lovely, but when I saw the lacy, sequined one, I couldn't resist. I picked it up by the hanger and took it off the rack so I could see it better. There wasn't much to it, I can tell you that. So as a joke, I held it up in front of me to show Brie and we laughed. I didn't touch more than the hip of the costume. I didn't even let it touch my clothing. I was respectful of it."

"Yet not enough to leave the damn thing alone." Olive couldn't help being the older sister for a moment. I'd have to thank her later.

The officer raised his head at this. He looked from Olive to me and smiled. He looked at Brie. It may have been with pity.

"This is what they do, Officer. This is what they do." Brie stifled a yawn.

"I see, Ms. V. We will want your fingerprints, as I'm sure they will find them on the clothes hanger and possibly the costume. If you could come to the station tomorrow, a technician will take your prints."

"As a teacher in the public schools in Maine and California, my prints are already in a database somewhere. If you can access them, it might be faster for you, but I'll come to the station in the morning if need be."

"Let me find out back at the station. Ms. Quirion has my card. Call in the morning and we will know if we need you to come in or not."

"Deal."

"Thank you for your time, ladies. We will be in touch if we need anything further from you. Have a good rest of your evening." He walked over to the female officer.

Dru and Stefan weren't anywhere in sight.

Brie rubbed her face. I took a deep breath. Olive was watching me.

"Your fingerprints are on that costume?! You know that makes you a suspect?! In a foreign country?!"

Fatigue was setting in so I wasn't my usual patient self. "How can I be a suspect by touching her flimsy costume? She wasn't strangled by it! And what was Dru going on about?" I wanted to know.

"I think he was just panicking when Stefan put his arm around him." Brie snuggled into the sofa cushions. "He couldn't get loose, and then he saw a police officer heading his way. That made it worse, and you caught his eye. He used you to deflect attention away from himself."

"But if he loves, er, loved Isabelle and he was sobbing on the phone, then why worry about the police and the manager and a costume on a hanger?"

"Let me repeat myself, I think he just panicked." Brie was getting exasperated with us. "The woman he loved just died in the arms of another man. He probably wasn't thinking all that clearly."

"Maybe," my small voice allowed.

Now Olive was showing signs of fatigue because she was stuck on me. "We'll probably learn more in the morning when you have your fingerprints taken at the police station."

"Or, smarty-pants, on the phone when Officer Williams tells me I don't need to go there."

"Well," Brie yawned wide and loud, "tomorrow will have to take care of itself. I'm done. I'm going back to the apartment to see what's on the news. You take your time with your sister. See you in the morning, Olive."

As she walked away, she turned to Olive, "Oh, and this is nothing like our usual vacations. You always bring spice to our lives, Olive. And I wouldn't have it any other way. Good night."

Olive smiled and her eyes teared up. Then she turned to me. "Now Vidalia, I don't want you to stay with me. I want you to do what you would usually do if it was just the two of you. I don't want to intrude or anything."

"I know, Olive. If I went with Brie right now, we would sit back and watch the news. She can do that and I can sit here and watch what happens with you until we get bored. We can also plan an adventure for tomorrow. Or maybe we just want a day by the water with a good book."

"Good book? No." Olive shook her head. "I didn't come here to get sunburned, and swimming can wait. What is there to do here?"

"Well, that stuff is in my three-ring binder for this trip."

Olive rolled her eyes knowingly.

"But I remember there is an arrowroot celebration. It's called a jollification—isn't that a great name for an event?"

Olive raised one eyebrow.

"Oh, you'd like this," I continued. "Arrowroot has medicinal qualities. It's good for kidney health. It has lots of B vitamins, too. Oh, and get this!" I snapped my fingers. "It can be used as an antidote to scorpion and some spider bites." I tilted my head toward her. "Maybe we should pack some when we're out in the jungle."

Olive gave me her deadpan expression. I was too much for my own good—too organized, too knowledgeable, and just too…*too*.

"First of all," she said, "of course you have your three-ring binder. You have an addiction to office supplies. I expect to see glitter dividers for different sections." She ticked off the section titles with her fingers. "Let's see—travel details, activities, and annual/monthly events including ecotourism, of course, of which foods and their medicinal qualities, are a part."

She shook a finger at me. "You better have one section for Brie's politics and business information. Second, no scorpion in its right mind would bite me if I was crazy enough to get near one. But just to be sure, how much of that dry powder do you have to swallow? I'd think you'd choke to death on it before the venom got to you. And third," she wagged a finger at me, "I do like the aid to digestion and B vitamins, parts. That's good to know for soups at the Grand, but it's also good to know in general. Where do we go for this jollification?"

"We can ask one of the activity people here, tomorrow." I said. "I also read that Vodou and Rastafari are two of the main religions here on Saint Martin. Are you up for learning about that from people who actually live those faiths? I don't know how we do that, but we can ask around. Especially after Bertrand took that amulet off his neck and put it on Isabelle. What do you think that was about? All I could think of were Vodou beliefs."

"You crack me up," Olive sputtered from her clenched teeth and pursed lips. She had been just letting me go on until I ran out of steam. "Brie was right. Here we go, making up a complete story from small bits of what we saw. We don't know if that was an amulet. It could be a piece of junk jewelry or a key to something or something completely different that they shared as children. And Vodou? Where did that come from? Maybe Rastafari beliefs. Oh my gosh. We're off and running. Well, it's been a long day of travel and excitement so I'm going to my apartment to wait for Coco."

"Yes, big sister, you're right." I stretched and yawned as I stood up. "We're into a new story of interest and intrigue. Oooh, the plot thickens. Like a good soup. Oh! Oh! I'm telling you, I could write these stories. Listen, have a good sleep. Call us tomorrow when you're ready for breakfast. We can walk just up the hill to the next resort and have breakfast there. They have a covered patio just above their pool. Anyway, give us a ring."

Olive walked down a hallway as I walked toward the elevator. Poor Isabelle. Poor Bertrand. And poor Dru, that crying dancer. And geez Louise, my fingerprints!

Stepping into the elevator, I was joined by a Caucasian American couple. They had been at the event, too.

"Honey," the man said to his wife, "we have no idea what killed that woman, but I think you're rushing to conclusions if you think it was terrorism with an airborne poison. C'mon, think a minute. Honey, take that scarf away from your face. The air is okay to breathe. She's the only one dead, and even the guy kissing her is still alive. He's fine, so airborne doesn't make sense. The authorities will figure it out, and we can read about it after we get home."

"Well," she said, "this is how things happen, you know." She unwound her scarf, crumpled it into one hand, and held the wad over her mouth. "First they murder one person and before you know it, it spreads. Oh, what if it's a virus and he had it on his lips or anything that touched her body anywhere? She was practically naked in that outfit." She straightened up, raised one eyebrow, and looked him in the eye. "Which I'm sure you were well aware of. He might have had a poison on him that transferred onto and into her skin and blood."

"Oh please, Margaret," the husband pleaded. "A poisonous blood transfer now? Maybe the woman just had a heart attack and died. No story. No mystery. You've got to start watching more sports and fewer medical shows on TV."

We all got out of the elevator on the same floor. The husband said good night and gave me an apologetic smile.

The devil in me couldn't be held back. I leaned toward the couple in a conspiratorial manner and whispered, "Vodou? Did you see that necklace he put on her?"

The woman gasped. The husband smacked his hand on his forehead and looked at me as he resigned himself to stay awake another hour while the wife jabbered about this new possibility. I walked toward my apartment with a big smile. Brie was going to love this story.

She was sitting out on the balcony sipping some tea. "Hi," and pointed to a second cup for me. And I smiled. With every cup she poured, I felt her love. We had learned to travel with our own green tea bags and sugar.

Then she looked out to the far corner of the beach. We hadn't been outside since Isabelle collapsed. Down the beach, we saw a fire burning. A crowd was gathered around it, but instead of the usual drinking, music, and dancing, it was quiet. Someone was speaking. Chanting? It was rhythmical and repetitive but in a language I didn't understand. Brie recognized that it was neither French nor Spanish but some language close to those. She couldn't understand what was being said, either. It sounded prayerful. The people standing around the fire began rocking from foot to foot as the chanting went on.

Something was thrown onto the fire and the flames shot upward, really high. More than a typical piece of wood would make, I thought.

"Wow, do you suppose that wood had something on it or in it to make the flame shoot up like that?"

Brie kept watching. "If it was wood," she said as she drank the last of her tea. She got up on her toes and kissed me on the cheek. I caught a smile on her lips as she walked inside.

"You and your stories, Vidalia. I'm looking forward to hear what you will come up with."

Chapter Eight

The four of us met in the lobby the next morning and walked up the hill for breakfast at the neighboring resort. It was already eighty degrees, and the hill was steep. We were all winded. As we waited for our coffee and tea, Coco shared what she learned with the medical team after Isabelle Simone had collapsed and died.

"Anaphylaxis. We know that's how she died but not what caused it. We ran all the blood tests for the usual allergies."

"Wait a second, Coco. How in the world were you allowed to stay with the medical team? You're a tourist from Alaska, for heaven's sake." Brie had to know.

"I kept my mouth shut at first, just doing whatever the doctor ordered. Checking vital signs, looking for abrasions, noting dilation of the eyes, checking the windpipe, that sort of thing. The man from the orphanage came by and asked for the money from her costume. I looked at the doctor. He looked at me and then gave me a little nod. The linens were giving us privacy so the doctor gently lifted each bra cup and checked for anything in the money or the materials that could be helpful. That's when I saw a cut under her breast and pointed it out. The doctor must have been impressed because he asked my name and details. I told him who I was and why I was here. Orphanage guy asked for the money and our hands were full with the body so we handed it to him and he left. I think the police took it from him for testing but I'm not sure."

"They did," Olive said. "We saw that happen in the lobby. So, how did you wrangle a seat in the ambulance?"

"I just stuck close to the doctor. His name, by the way, is Carl Van Heusen. When he climbed into his car, I just looked at him like a kid wanting to go with a superhero. He took pity on me. I know he did because he looked down at the ground so I couldn't see his smile. He looked up and asked if I was coming or not. Man, oh man. I was in that front seat slicker 'n snot, baby. So, yes. I became a visitor to the medical team."

She took a breath. "I think it was because I'm attending the conference on Saba that got me in. As I was saying, we tested everything we could think of." Then Coco clapped her hands a little and said in a soft but excited voice, "I ordered my Saint Martin Hospital scrubs before I left last night."

So Coco. I clapped for her happiness.

"But anyway." Her face became somber as she wrapped her hand around her water glass. "Something got into her system and her body just shut down and quit. She had that single thin cut under one breast, almost like a paper cut that looked fresh and inflamed, but that was it."

Olive put her napkin in her lap. "Probably a paper cut from those filthy dollar bills she kept stuffing in her bra all night." She looked off to one side. "Remember when Isabelle winced? That's probably when it happened."

"That's why I never put cash in my bra," I stated. "These almost AAs are too fragile."

Olive splurted tea out of her mouth. "That and the cash would just fall right out the bottom." She looked at Coco and Brie, neither of whom had ever experienced small breasts. "A sister knows these things."

Brie concentrated on her menu. She was biting her lip.

Coco puffed out her chest. "These 38 CCCs can hold cash, kids' toys, and snacks all day. Nothing gets past these babies. They're like Fort Knox."

Now Brie was blushing over the menu. Her shoulders were starting to go up and down. "I can't believe this is the breakfast conversation at a restaurant! You three crack me up." She looked around. "Where is that coffee? I could use a good swig."

Picking up where she left off, Olive continued, "And that dancer boyfriend—Dru, wasn't it? He did it." She put both hands flat on the table and leaned in. "That's probably where and how she was exposed to the poison."

"Oh, here we go," said Brie, looking skyward. "And they're off."

Coffee and tea arrived, and we gave our breakfast orders. The covered porch where we sat overlooked an infinity pool that led our eyes out to the ocean. Heaven. A few sunbathers were already lounging around the pool with their visors, books, and water bottles.

Coco stirred cream into her coffee. "I'm impressed with the medical system here. The island hospital is great. It has everything they might need. And for a little island in the middle of a big ocean, that can be a lot."

She took a sip of her coffee. "Since this is a pretty high visibility and unusual death they're moving the body to the Saba Medical Center for further examination." She rubbed her hands together in excitement. "The hospital here is like some of the hospitals in Alaska. Most doctors at home are still mostly white men, and those that aren't get treated differently. Not open hostility, but a sense of questioning of their decisions and diagnoses. Not here. Last night, everyone from the guy pushing a gurney to the head of the forensic team was treated with respect and given their authority."

Coco took another sip of her coffee. "They didn't simply treat Isabelle as a dead body. They learned which religion she had been brought up with and whether she currently observed. They didn't just assume everyone was Christian. She was, but isn't it cool that that's one of the first questions? The autopsy will take place on Saba, so I might get more information when my conference starts on Monday. And get this…"

Coco took a good swallow of her coffee and looked out over the pool to the sea. Her face became angelic, as if she had been captured by the view. "This place is magnificent. The ocean off the coast of Alaska doesn't look like this."

"Coco, come back to us." Olive patted her hand. "What are we supposed to get, honey?"

"What? Oh, right. Well, when some of the nurses were out of earshot of the doctors, they were talking about Isabelle being brought up in the Catholic religion. A few others were making comments about the death being related to some belief or myth. When they heard about the animal sound, one of them actually shuddered and pulled a necklace out from under her scrubs and kissed an amulet or maybe stone figure hanging from it."

"What's that all about?" Olive asked. "People last night looked toward that awful screech as if it had some meaning. Brie, you heard that a seer may have sacrificed that animal to help Isabelle cross into paradise."

A waiter had brought our breakfasts to the table and waited as Olive finished. The young man had medium-brown skin, black slacks, and a yellow resort shirt with the logo on the breast pocket. He hesitated, not putting the dishes on the table but not turning away, either. We all looked at him. He finally put the breakfasts on the table and rocked back and forth from his heels to his toes.

"Is everything all right?" I asked.

"I apologize, ladies. You are talking about Isabelle Simone's death last night, I think." He looked around the room quickly. We nodded yes and he went on, "She was ahead of me all through school. She became known for her voice, dancing and friendly disposition. She was nice to everyone. Isabelle was also very smart, for a girl."

A chill rippled around our table. None of us looked at the others. Most of us just let it go.

Coco asked, "How was she smart, for a girl, I mean?"

"She was good in science. She beat Bertrand in their fifth grade science fair with one of her chemical experiments. Oooh, Bertrand was extra smart, especially in science. So when he was beat by a girl, he was at odds. Ooh, he got teased! What could he do?" The waiter looked at each of us. We sat there.

"Bertrand started to sing and dance, you know? To beat her at her own game. And he was good." The waiter looked a bit surprised.

"All through high school, competitions between them went on. Each one winning and each one losing. When they were competing, the auditoriums were filled with spectators cheering for their favorite."

He lowered his voice. "Some small bets were made now and then, too. But they were both good kids. I looked up to both of them. Sometimes they would team up, you know? Work and perform together for fundraisers or special island events. Mmmm, those were magical times, I tell you. When they sang "The Periodic Table Song" as a love duet, people came undone! We couldn't tell if they loved science or each other. They left it up to us, and boy, didn't the rumors fly!" His eyes were sparkling.

This guy had the story of the day! "So what happened to them?" I prodded.

"As all good things go," he continued, "they grew up and both followed their fates. Isabelle developed into a beauty, and what does a beautiful girl become if the gods look kindly on her? A dancer and singer with men ogling her and other girls admiring her. What more could a woman want?"

Coco, our Alaskan bush nurse and mother of three, let out a low growl. "She could have become a mother or wife."

"Isabelle knew that marriage or her fun with science would not give her the life she could have with performing, so she left all that behind. Bertrand also saw that he was unlikely to become a headliner. He would be limited to backing up the beautiful women, so he focused on science. So you see, in the end, each went back to their calling. What you saw last evening was Bertrand's second hustle. His career is as a scientist at the water desalination plant." He pointed to our glasses of water. "You might thank him for that water you are drinking, eh?"

"Wowza," I said. "That is a lot of story. Thank you for telling us about those two."

Brie took up the reins after the waiter left. "Enough of that. First off today, Vidalia has to call the police station and the answer will influence the rest of the day. It might be a good day to go to Phillipsburg and the open market. Olive, the different stalls will have every kind of herb and seasoning for soups that you could ask for. I'll get to practice my French, and we can eat some great food for lunch."

"Then," I added, "if we have the energy, we can shop at Le Grande Marche, that grocery store near the rotary. The one with all the European cheeses, incredible fruits—and oh, maybe they'll have wine samples. I love this island."

"Find us down on the beach after your call to the police station and we can skedaddle and have some fun." Olive stood up and was ready to head back down the hill.

Brie and I returned to our apartment and called the police station, asking for Officer Williams. After we waited on hold, a woman came onto the line.

"Good morning, Ms. V. Ahern, my name is Detective Pamela Poissonier. I understand you are calling Officer Williams regarding your need to supply this department with your fingerprints. I also understand that you were seen holding the costume Ms. Simone was wearing when she collapsed. I have a note here indicating that your fingerprints were received from the State of Maine Department of Education overnight and we have them here. You will not be needed here at the precinct."

"Woo-hoo!" I was happy.

"However, Ms. V. Ahern, I must ask you to remain accessible to this department as a possible investigation may be underway."

"What does that mean? Accessible? Can I do touristy things? Can I even go to, let's say, Saba for a day if we feel like it?" I didn't like the sounds of this.

"You are welcome to participate in any activities of your choosing. We have Ms. Brie Quirion's email address from her statement to Officer Williams. We will contact you via your apartment at the resort and Ms. Quirion's email."

"Can you tell me what you might need me for? I mean, this is sounding a little creepy." I definitely wasn't liking the way this was going.

"Ms. V Ahern, a woman died last night and you were seen handling her costume and those of others. Every possible lead is being investigated. We will contact you if we need anything further from you. For now, I suggest you return to your list of attractions and leave this investigation to us. Are there any other questions?"

I knew a conversation snapping shut when I heard it.

"Ah, no, ma'am."

"It's Detective Poissonier."

"All right then, Detective Poissonier. I have no further questions. I'll just go and have fun with my friends. You be safe and have a nice day. Goodbye." I hung up.

"That is one straightforward badass detective. I hope I stay out of her crosshairs."

Brie came and sat by me. "From what I overheard, they have my email address so they can contact you if they need to. That sounds simple enough."

"It does, doesn't it? Yet, I still feel a little like a suspect." I turned to Brie. "I picked up a piece of cloth and now I have to be available? This doesn't feel good."

"Don't make this more than it is. This is our first full day here. You've gotten your business call taken care of. Now let's go and walk in the sun and be tourists. Try to put all of this aside for now." Brie took my hand as she stood up and pulled me up with her.

She gave me a reassuring hug and a little kiss.

"Let's go get your sister and Coco and explore the open market in Phillipsburg. That sounds more like why we came here, doesn't it?"

"You're right. I'll just throw some things in my shoulder tote and I'm ready."

We found Coco and Olive under a palm tree, watching people in the surf and birds flying by.

"Well, here we are. I don't have to go and have my fingerprints taken so we can go anytime." I re-shouldered my bag.

Coco and Olive said, "Let's go!" and we went.

Chapter Nine

I drove the midsize rental car and maneuvered through the rotary traffic at the bottom of the hill by the desalination plant. One can't be skittish driving in Saint Martin. Lots of people walk, and sidewalks aren't always available. Whether it is from the bus stop to work and home or from a bus stop to shopping, people are walking at a pace commensurate with highly humid eighty-degree heat and sunshine that doesn't quit. Add free-roaming chickens, roosters, and an occasional goat to the vehicles, from scooters to construction trucks, and you better be concentrating if you are behind the wheel in a rental car.

We arrived in Phillipsburg midmorning. The open market was already bustling. Cruise-ship passengers swarmed the streets and shops. As soon as we stepped out of the car, the smell of exhaust, the noises of the market women negotiating with customers, and the backup beeps from delivery and construction trucks hit us in a wave.

I had my hat and sunblock on. I was ready to go. I gave a reusable bag to Coco, Brie, and Olive, keeping one for myself, for our treasures. Unfortunately for Brie, the government building was closed on Saturday, so she sauntered over toward the market with the rest of us, eager to immerse herself in the language.

At one of the first stalls, gallon containers of saffron, cayenne, cumin, turmeric, and ginger sent Olive into a frenzy. The colors were so robust and the quantities luxurious. She bought a prepackaged sampler in the cutest straw box with a palm tree embroidered on it. "Oh, this is exactly why I came here!" Her smile was as big as the island.

The clothing stalls caught my attention but my frugality won out, for the moment.

Olive walked over to a stall full of skirts and scarves. A woman was rearranging, folding, and rehanging scarves from a heap left by an earlier group. She wasn't smiling.

"Hello," Olive said to her. "Your scarves are beautiful. I promise I won't make a mess of them." The woman smiled and nodded.

Olive wiped her hands on her shorts before touching a single scarf. Seafoam-green, aqua, and deep-purple scarves draped over the counter and swayed in the breeze created by passersby. Navel-orange, canary-yellow, and kelly-green scarves hung from high on one wall. Scarves of cranberry red and persimmon orange with bursts of white hung below them. Olive backed up to one wall and covered herself in the colors. Her face was bright pink and glowing. She was a chameleon. She giggled with delight.

Drawn to all shades of green, Olive swept around the eight-by-eight-foot stall. All those dance lessons at Alice Hanley's Dance Studio were not wasted. Reaching up on tiptoe toward hanging scarves and swooping low to those on the counter, she created a breeze so they would flutter. Olive left the scarves in place so as not to trouble the woman. Her name tag read "Bridget."

"Bridget, is it all right if I hold a few scarves up to my face to see how they look?" She turned to Brie. "Brie, can you help me ask? You speaking French will be clearer than my attempts to ask questions."

Brie stepped up and introduced herself and explained who we were, where we were from, and why we were there. She described Olive's collection of scarves at home in Maine and how she wanted one of Bridget's scarves to enhance her collection. Of course, all of this was in French, but I have traveled enough with Brie to understand cultural norms and the value of friendly banter.

Bridget said, "I understand and speak enough English for this work but French is my first language. Thank you for learning my language."

Bridget grinned and turned to Olive. Bridget began draping scarves over and around Olive. Brie had magically changed the picture of us as loud Americans into well-meaning people on the trip of their lives with her well-honed language and cultural skills.

Olive held scarves to her neck and cheeks with one hand and a mirror in the other until she found her scarf. We all oohed and aahed at her choice. We caught her giddiness. She hugged Bridget. Bridget chuckled.

Olive was laughing hysterically by now. She twirled the scarf in the air and took a feeble leap. "I'm a ribbon dancer!"

"You get a ten for enthusiasm!"

She wrapped it low on her hips and made a round, swiveling move. "I'm a belly dancer!"

"All you need are some finger cymbals," Coco laughed.

A man, graying at his temples and moustache, had been standing at the next stall, watching. I had the feeling he'd been enjoying our antics, but by now he was so amused he simply dropped all pretense, watched, and smiled.

Laying her scarf over her head, then wrapping it around her neck and finally over her mouth, Olive said, "I'm a secret agent, and I have you under surveillance. Oh, Vidalia! Approach me for a clandestine meeting and we'll have a code phrase."

Olive and I stealthily walked toward each other. She uncovered her face enough to say, "Tiger flies at midnight."

"Under the spreading chestnut tree," I whispered out of the side of my mouth.

Brie and Coco were begging us to stop, they were laughing so hard.

"Where do you two come up with this stuff?"

The man chuckled out loud and quickly put his closed fist up to his mouth to stifle himself. The four of us turned toward him. Picture The Three Stooges in their "Niagara Falls" routine. The poor man went pale and just as quickly abandoned his self-restraint. He smiled broadly and dropped his arms by his sides in open acceptance of being caught eavesdropping on our fun.

"Thank you, ladies. I have been enjoying your frivolity. I hope I haven't intruded."

He walked closer, directly toward Olive. She crossed one arm across her day pack in defense mode against a possible theft but kept a smaller smile on her face. He may have noticed but didn't take his eyes off her.

"I agree that this scarf compliments you," he said as he ran his index finger over the scarf still around Olive's neck. "The colors bring out your eyes, and the design appears to bring out your spirit."

Olive gave him her deadpan look but didn't budge. "Why, thank you, sir."

He caught the chill and doubled down.

"You sway like a palm tree." His hips swayed. One of Olive's eyebrows shot up but again, she didn't move away. Coco, Brie, and I stood still and just watched. This was better than anything we could have made up.

Undeterred, perhaps even further motivated, he went on, "My name is Adrien Bemuse and I work at this market. Bridget knows me to be a gentleman, don't you, Bridget?"

Lifting her head from her folding, "Oh yes, Mr. Bemuse." She lowered it again but kept an eye on what was happening.

Adrien turned back to Olive. "And you are?"

"Just visiting."

"I see that you are protective of your privacy and applaud you for that. But clearly, I am no threat to you. I'm merely offering you another person's opinion of a scarf. Doesn't this happen in America?"

Olive started to unwrap the scarf from her head and neck. She laid it on Bridget's counter. She could go either way on this. She fingered the scarf. She looked up at Adrien. Her eyes flickered. "Is there a different scarf that you feel suits me?"

I gasped. I whispered to Brie and Coco, "Was that a gauntlet I just heard hit the ground?"

Adrien let out a cool breath as he began a sweep of Bridget's stall. Bridget pointed out a few scarves for him to consider. He came back to the chosen scarf and lifted it. "I like this one very much but it lacks something. Bridget, could we have the slightest thread of shimmer added to this one? Miss Just Visiting has the flow and colors, but she is showing me that there is a sparkle that this scarf does not portray. Could we adjust this scarf in a short time?"

Olive blushed. She breathed. She nodded.

"Yes, Mr. Bemuse." Bridget took the scarf. "I can make that adjustment in just a few minutes. Perhaps the ladies would like to have a drink nearby and come back when they are finished?"

The mention of a cold drink had me salivating. We all needed to get into the shade, off our feet.

Olive started to take out money, but Bridget stopped her. "Oh no, Madame. You can pay later, only if you like it."

"Oh, okay. That's great. Thank you, Bridget. And not a lot of sparkle. I get overwhelmed."

Bridget patted Olive's hand.

Adrien Bemuse had left.

We walked along the restaurant-lined boardwalk and marveled at the street performers until we settled on an establishment that fit all of our wants: crisp salads, ice-cold beverages, tapas, and live music. We sat at a table with a large umbrella keeping the sun from a direct hit on our northern, white skin. When we took our hats off, Olive's and my bird-feather-thin hair stuck to our heads. A little finger fluffing made us feel better but didn't really help our appearance. Brie always wears a visor and has natural wavy hair, so she looked fine. Coco's full, floppy brimmed hat not only shielded her freckled whiteness but kept all of those thick curls in check. As soon as she removed her hat, the frizzing began.

A steel band played and offered their CDs for sale. The wind was mild, the grilling fish crackled in the open-air cook area. We were happy campers.

We were still laughing and replaying parts of Olive's exchange with the mysterious but beguiling Adrien Bemuse.

To our surprise, our waiter was Dru, the dancer, the stuffer of money, he-who-threw-suspicion-on-me, and Coco's dancer from last night. He barely glanced at our faces. He played his part as a seaside grill waiter with a life of surf, sand, and music as the only pieces of his life. Of course, the four of us couldn't suppress the fact that we recognized him.

Coco, who missed Dru throwing me under the bus last night, remembered her dance with him. "Hello, sweetheart!" She shook her shoulders and luscious tatas at him with a big grin. He definitely looked right at her. Then a slow smile crept onto his face.

"Ah yes, my favorite dancing partner from last night."

I'll bet he uses that line a lot. Then he actually looked at the rest of us. He stopped short when he got to me.

"Uh, hi again." I waved my fingers at him. "We also met last night but under different circumstances. First, you yelled at me for touching the costumes and then you got the police to spend time with me while you were carted off onto the patio by your manager."

"Yes, well, I am sorry you were delayed longer than most. But when I saw the detective come toward me and the manager had me in a hold, I panicked. Plain and simple. Of course, I am not involved in poor Isabelle's death, but in those moments I was frightened so when you came into view, I used you to get them off me. Again, I'm sorry."

"Well, I did have to furnish my fingerprints but other than that, no harm done." I paused. "I'm sorry Isabelle died. I saw how upset you were when you walked through the lobby and texted on your phone."

One of Dru's eyebrows pitched upward, and he looked at me suspiciously.

I started to babble my way out of trouble. Never a good strategy, but my first in a line of equally ineffective default behaviors.

"Oh, I'm not a detective or anything. And I didn't mean to spy on you last night. We were just sitting in the lobby as everyone left the patio and we saw you among the other people. And we noticed how sad you looked and acted. It must have been a terrible shock, probably still is. I hope that phone call you made and the talk with the manager helped."

Now Dru was looking at me with incredulity and increasing suspicion.

Olive put her hand on my forearm. "Vidalia, why don't we just let Dru do his job? Dru, forgive my sister, she is always looking for a story, even if she has to make one up."

Dru took our drink orders and walked away.

"I know, I know." I held up both hands in surrender. "I was just acting like a nosy, noisy American who doesn't respect the boundaries of others. I'll apologize when and if he comes back. I'm sorry."

Coco said, "Well, we could ask him more questions if he comes back. Maybe he wants to talk about what happened."

Olive was quick. "To a group of American strangers?! I don't think so." She ducked her head and lowered her voice. "Although, I would love to know more."

Brie pretended she hadn't heard us and kept her eyes on the steel drum players. She was recording them on her iPad. Dru came back carrying our drinks. Brie walked over and bought a CD.

"Dru," I started, "I apologize for talking about last night, especially while you're working. I didn't mean to upset you, and again, I'm sorry about your friend."

Dru set our drinks in front of us with a practiced pace; not too quickly, setting them quietly down on the brushed metal table top. "I accept your apology, madam. Last night was the sudden end of many things. It was not supposed to be. Isabelle Simone will never sing again, and that is a loss. I was her best and favored dancer."

He put his hands in the pockets of his apron. "I traveled with her when she toured other islands and countries. Isabelle and I were very close, as you say in America. So last night was the last time I held her in my arms. So yes, you see, I am sad it all came to an unfortunate end last night."

The four of us were quiet.

Dru smiled. "You Americans become so sad at death. I am sad that I will miss Isabelle until I see her again in the afterlife, but I am not sad that she has died. We all die at some point. Isabelle died while she was performing. It is what she loved to do most. She died happy." His hands were twisting in those pockets. "I will continue to perform. It will be different, but I will still sing and dance. In that way, I can keep Isabelle with me."

He took a beat.

"Perhaps your pity on me might lead you to help me get a performing gig in America."

He may have been half-joking. Always working toward the end goal.

Brie sprang into one of her speeches. Selling the state of Maine was something she did regularly.

"Well, we have the Maine State Music Theatre and the Ogunquit Playhouse, the Theater at Monmouth, too. Oh, we have some wonderful places to perform. Oh, and Lakewood, near us. But remember, we live in Maine—you may want to get a look at a map before you get on a plane."

"I have not heard of those places. I know of Las Vegas and New York City and Los Angeles. Also, you have Branson, Missouri, right? Those places have a lot of performers like me."

"Yes, they do. It seems to me you could contact someone. Let me think about that as we eat, and I'll try to have a contact for you before we leave."

"Really?! That could happen? Okay!"

My nosiness pushed through. "May I ask you about that animal screeching that some people heard and looked towards? Did that have some specific meaning?"

He looked from side to side. "For those who believe, the sound was probably an animal being sacrificed, probably by a *houngnan*, one of our Vodou priests, to appease the gods. When I heard it, I prayed that the way was being opened for Isabelle to move quickly and peacefully into the afterlife."

Brie asked, "But how could someone have known ahead of time to 'open' this portal? We heard the sound at just about the same time Isabelle dropped to the floor."

"Ah," Dru said, "our *houngnan* sometimes know things."

Brie clicked her iPad to life.

"Dru," I asked, "one more question before we order. We don't want to get you in trouble with your boss for taking too much time with us."

"Yet, you're still talking," Olive jibed.

I ignored her. "Last night, Brie and I saw a bonfire down the beach. The people looked as though they were chanting and maybe dancing in rhythm? And then, one of them tossed something onto the fire that caused a whoosh of flame. Can you tell us about that?"

Dru looked over toward the bar and made eye contact with a man I guessed was the boss. Dru nodded at him, the man nodded back, and Dru turned back toward us. "The boss is my brother, and he lets me work when I'm home between tours. Once word was around the island of Isabelle's death, my brother knew I would be here today earning money one way or another."

"There are many religions on the island of Saint Martin. You may have seen some Rastafarians celebrating the life that had just passed. Rastis love living a full life and may have been celebrating the spirit that was here. The whoosh, as you say, was a chemical they put on their wood to create a dramatic effect, possibly to climax the celebration of Isabelle's life." He lowered and shook his head. "All of our plans. Gone."

Dru exhaled, slapped his hands together, and put them on his hips.

"Now I will tell you about our luncheon specials. Of course, you will want our delicious seafood with mango salsa and a side salad with jicama. We have a Jamaican jerk chicken with curried carrots and a chilled fruit soup or a fruit kabob on a bed of cottage cheese. I will deliver a basket of rolls to the table with our house-made herbed goat cheese. Shall I bring another round of drinks while you make your decisions?"

"Oh no," we all said at the same time.

Olive said, "We'll order now. We've been here longer than we planned as it is." We all ordered, being sure to order at least one of every special so we could taste-test everything.

The steel drum players were playing familiar pop tunes with a tropical flair. "I Can See Clearly Now" never sounded so light and playful. I softly sang along with the band. Brie and I smartly alternated sips of water with sips of wine. We wanted endurance as a factor in our time on the island. Guzzling a glass of wine would lead me to a nap back home, and that wasn't on my agenda. Passersby stopped to listen to the band, and a few danced. Everyone was smiling and getting along. The female detective from last night walked by. She must have been on a break.

Dru delivered our food. "Now, ladies, here you have the finest and freshest food on the island. Enjoy the tastes and textures. I'll be back to check on you in a little bit, okay?" Before we could respond, he was over with the band, singing and dancing.

We were taking in the visual effects of our food. Coco took a few photos to send back to her Alaskan colleagues. "This will make them drool. Just the sweat on the glasses will make them laugh. We don't get a lot of sweating glassware in Alaska." She put her phone away. "I think Dru has had enough of us. He seems to switch into performance mode quickly. Look at him over there. He's dancing with everyone!"

"Action is the distraction," Olive said.

Brie added, "You don't make any money crying. I'm emailing the office for help with getting Dru a foot in the door in the States. This will be new for me."

Large shrimp had been skewered and grilled over the wood fire, glazed with butter, garlic, and herbs. A whitefish had been dipped in coconut and grilled to a sweet, crisp deliciousness. My New England palate doesn't take hot peppers well at all. I don't think food should hurt. The mango salsa was delicious, but the peppers in it allowed me only a taste. The other three practically lapped the plate clean. Long, thin strips of chicken had been grilled with jerk seasonings.

Those curried carrots were addictive. I dipped mine in the cottage cheese. "Oh my," I said. "If we made a platter of these carrots and had a yogurt, dill, and cucumber dip, people would love us even more than they already do."

Nods of agreement came from around the table. No one stopped eating.

Olive said, "I don't usually like cold soup, but this is good. What do you think is in it, Brie?"

Brie said, "Well, let's see. It's a little thick and I don't taste any dairy, which is good for this temperature. So what's the thickener? Banana?"

We spoke out when we identified a taste.

"I taste the mango," Brie said.

Coco said, "I taste and feel the coconut."

"It's too watery to be a smoothie but too thick to be a juice drink," I said. "Arrowroot for the thickener, Olive?"

"Hoo-boy," she said, "you kill me."

"What are the seasonings? Is that cinnamon?" Coco asked.

"Vanilla?" Brie added.

"There's something else. Something we don't usually use—cardamom?" I said, "I don't even know what cardamom tastes like, but I do enjoy saying the word. And, Olive." I inserted into my little speech because she was rolling her eyes at me. "It could be cardamom. Right, Brie?" I asked, looking for backup. Brie once again pretended she hadn't heard me.

"Cardamom? You're a dope."

"Ladies? Forgive my interruption, but I wanted to deliver your scarf."

It was Bridget! She handed Olive a small gift bag. Olive took the tissue-wrapped parcel and unfolded the scarf. Her scarf.

"Oh!" She put one hand over her mouth. "It's perfect." She lifted the scarf so the breeze caught it. Her eyes puddled.

"Oh, Olive. That Adrien knows his stuff. He had your energy pegged to the details, didn't he?" Coco touched the scarf. "It's you."

Pulling herself together, Olive reached into her pack for her money and again, Bridget stopped her. "Mr. Bemuse has taken care of the cost. He hopes you accept this as a token of the high regard he has for you." She was smiling wide at this ongoing game.

"You are kidding me. My, my, my, that guy has guts. Where is he?"

"He has left for the day."

"Must be nice to work a half-day." Olive cleared her throat. "Will you please thank Mr. Bemuse for me?" She tossed her head back as she flung the scarf around her neck. "And tell him that I will always treasure our few moments together."

"Game on!" Coco laughed into her drink.

Bridget left, and we marveled over the subtlety in the fabric.

Dru came to the table with our check.

Brie asked, "Dru, why don't you type in your contact information so someone in the congressman's office can let you know what we find out? I'm wondering about the visas or a green card to get you started. This is new for me, but I like the chance to do this."

Dru took the iPad and got all of his contact information onto it. "Thank you very much, Ms. Quirion. This would be a chance of a lifetime."

"Okay, I'll email you later today so you have my address. Let's be sure to stay in touch." She smiled and shook his hand. He was bouncing from foot to foot.

"Hey Dru, this has been quite the lunch. Tell us, will you? What is the mystery flavor in that soup?" Coco asked as she fished her credit card from her pocket.

"Lime and coconut milk," Dru accepted her card and left to process it.

"If it's all the same to everyone, can we just rotate paying for meals and figure it will all work out in the end?" she offered.

We were all good with that.

Dru returned. Coco took care of the tip and we were ready to move.

"Well, everything was delicious, and this is just our first lunch here. Oh, this is good." I stood and stretched.

Olive suggested we walk around the nearby courtyard of shops just to see what was there. We breezed by the tourist souvenir shops crowded with cruise-ship passengers. We watched a surf-shop worker giving a surfing lesson on the beach. Off in a corner was a little, stuffed bookstore that almost didn't fit with the rest of the courtyard.

The proprietress was giving orders into her headset phone while straightening books and shelving others. Her tone allowed zero challenge from whoever she was ordering around on the other end of the line. My nosy ears heard "funeral, celebration of great magnitude, the best from the food vendors and none of their second-rate chicken." I nudged Olive's ribs and rolled my eyes in the woman's direction.

"Tssst," my sister hissed. "Mind your own business and give the woman her privacy."

I took a business card from the counter before we left.

Going out the door, I saw the detective coming in! The store owner had finished her call, and the two women started talking. The detective was taking notes.

As soon as we were out in the courtyard again, Olive turned to me and asked, "What did that woman say about a funeral of great magnitude?"

"Oh, so much for minding my own business," I responded. I told her what I'd heard. "Well, how many funerals are there being planned on this island today, especially one of great magnitude? It must be for Isabelle. Maybe that woman is, let me think, Isabelle's poor mother."

Brie kept walking by us as she added, "Or maybe the woman was talking about a book. You know, she is running a bookstore. You two never stop."

"Really, well, Brie," stammered Olive as she turned toward me, building up steam.

"Let's connect the dots, Vidalia." She stuck out her thumb. "A woman sings and dances with her lead backup dancer, Dru, who obviously loved her." Her index finger popped out from her fist. "She dances and sings with her childhood competition, Bertrand, but I think they were in love. The smoldering kind. Smoldering lover kisses her and she drops dead." She opened her hand and flopped it toward the ground.

"But that comes just after money has been slipped under her boobs in her costume," I offered.

Back came Olive's hand with three fingers up. "The medical team found a cut under one breast that looked irritated. The cause of death was anaphylaxis." She thrust her thumb down the beach. "We hear chickens being sacrificed and see bonfires burning." All fingers and thumb were counting a full five. "Isabelle was a devout Catholic."

"And now," both hands were splayed at the ends of her outstretched arms. "there's a woman in a bookstore arranging a funeral of great magnitude to celebrate the life of, who? Probably Isabelle. That's all I'm saying. Who else on this island is deserving of the best chicken, huh?" She cocked her head.

Brie looked at me. "Have I told you how much I love your family?"

"Many times," I smiled.

"Let's go." Brie shook her head slowly and chuckled, "We still have grocery shopping to do."

"How long can that take?" Coco asked.

"Just wait," I said.

Le Grande Marche was near the rotary on our way back to the resort. Very European. The cheese selection—smoked baby Gouda being my favorite—made me swoon. We purchased staples for daily breakfasts in the apartments with light meals, snacks, and beverages throughout the days. Olive and Coco oohed and aahed their way through the aisles, seeing different brands of common items from around the world. We studied and discussed unfamiliar items as we decided to try or pass on them. One full corner of the store was the liquor, beer, and wine section. Yes, there were samples available. You don't see that in the States. Brie, Coco, and I sampled enough to make a couple of wine and beer selections. We waddled out of the store laden down with more food than we probably would need but happy all the same.

Back at the Peacock, we put away our purchases, including the herbs Olive had picked up at the outdoor market in Phillipsburg, changed into swimsuits, and hit the beach.

There is nothing, nothing, I tell you, like walking straight into the Caribbean Ocean and diving underwater without the familiar head freeze of the Atlantic off the coast of Maine. The Caribbean is actually the color of that Crayola crayon labeled "seafoam green." And you can float for as long as you want, not for as long as you can stand it. Then you can walk out of the water to your towel and not shiver. I believe this is one of life's greatest gifts to me.

By now, all four of us were pooped from travel and the excitement since we had arrived. We had a simple dinner of nacho chips with cheese and salsa out on our balcony with a glass of our new wine with ice cream for dessert. Then we were all ready for some sound sleep, with dreams of dancers and Vodou.

Chapter Ten

Sunday morning, a quiet time because of all the churchgoers and late sleepers. We started at the breakfast buffet in our shorts, jerseys, and hats. Our arms, legs, and sandaled feet were already well oiled or SPF 50'd. There was no talk of the death, less than a day and a half ago.

Neon-colored flyers for snorkeling, glass-bottomed boat rides, and a submarine ride were prominently displayed near every food and drink stand. The concierge was chatting with guests, encouraging different activities throughout the island. It was a happy time.

I've never been a sun bunny, so I bee lined it to a table built around the trunk of a palm tree. Olive joined me while Brie and Coco languished in the sun. Brie is from French-Canadian lineage, so her skin browns nicely. Coco, on the other hand, is a freckled, almost red-haired woman, so she was in jeopardy of burning every second she was out there. And she's a nurse and knows better. But she lives in Alaska. So maybe it balanced out.

The fruits were so fresh and juicy, my mouth watered just looking at them. A mound of those, a little granola, and a café au lait were perfect. We absorbed the heat. The sun and sound of the waves became a magical background while we were swept away by our books or wave-watching.

For lunch, we walked over to the casino next to the resort. We were usually too frugal to gamble, so this was an adventure. The casino was nearly empty of customers. Brie and I sidled up to a table for a game of twenty-one.

Never having played this in a casino, I asked for a tutorial from the smiling and encouraging dealer. A few other women our age joined us, and before long, we were laughing so hard that others gathered around to watch and cheer us on.

Janet from Chicago appeared to enjoy saying "Hit me" to the dealer because she went way over twenty-one on every hand she played. She was laughing so much, she had to cross her legs. Betty from Charlotte kept saying, "Oh, mah sister is never goin' ta believe Ahh did this! The Prayer Circle at church will be prayin' for a year over this, but it's just so much fun and y'all are so nice."

Brie was seriously trying to figure out if she should take a card or hold. I could hear her muttering under her breath, "Two jacks already on the table, one of them is mine." She's a competitor, that one.

Not me. I eyeballed my cards and even looked at what the other players had on the table before giving a half-hearted guess about taking another card or not.

Whoever won a round would whoop as though she had just won the Triple Crown, and the rest would over-moan in their agony of defeat. "Come on, baby needs new shoes!" was shouted a few times. We must have all seen the same movies to learn our gambling jargon. With two-dollar bets and whooping and hollering, we had a terrifically memorable time, and I only lost ten dollars. My limit.

Olive and Coco were at the slot machines with their rolls of coins. Coco, whose motto was go big or go home, played the half-dollar and dollar slots. Olive found a penny slot and worked her way up from there. She allowed herself one roll each of pennies, nickels, and dimes and when those were gone, she would be done. She won small amounts to keep her going, and even she had to admit that she had fun. For us, it was a wild time.

The piped-in music was light and playful. A dining balcony overlooked the beach. Turquoise tables had chairs with cantaloupe-orange seats, purple backs, and cobalt accents that set a worry-free zone tone. As we ordered, we saw music equipment being set up inside.

"Ladies, if we lived here," I said, "we would never have to shovel again."

Brie added, "Wouldn't need down-filled parkas."

Olive corrected, "They use Thinsulate now. It's more slimming. That's so important in the frigid, icy weather—looking slim."

"To some," Coco tossed out.

"I could stop feigning interest in going snowshoeing or cross-country skiing," I said with relief.

"What is the equivalent here of slipping on ice? That flailing of arms and legs trying to remain upright and wrenching my back," Olive wondered aloud. "I would almost miss that."

"Like a migraine headache," I offered.

"We have snow days at home," Coco said. "Do you think they have heat days here?"

Brie stated, "They have hurricanes. A lot more homes have their roofs peeled off in the high winds than we have crash in from the weight of snow."

"There is our cup of reality. Thanks for raining on my fantasy," I said.

It was effective.

"I would miss the seasons," Brie said.

"Especially the spring greens and fall colors," Olive added.

"Yes, but don't forget our mud season, flu season, and the never-ending football season."

"Go Patriots!"

"Yes, by all means, go Pats! But couldn't they go a little more quickly and not delay the Sunday evening television shows?" I lamented.

"There's the rub," Brie said. "It isn't football but anything that gets in the way of your TV viewing."

"Well, it is an imposition and a disappointment. Everyone else stays within their time slots. It's accountability."

"Ah, there's the real irritation for you, Vidalia, isn't it?" Olive challenged. "You're not in control when the football game delays your scheduled TV time."

"How much do you charge for that psychobabble insight, my dear *older* sister?"

"Oh nothing, my dear, simple sister. Chalk it up to unconditional love and support."

"Mom always liked you best."

"Do you blame her?"

Brie and Coco applauded our performance.

All at once, we heard "Day-O!" and a band strike up "The Banana Boat Song." We looked inside and there was Donna, the backup singer from our first night. It was odd to see a powder-blue satin gown with ivory sequin trim at two o'clock in the afternoon, but what did I know? We weren't regulars in a casino. Donna performed to the near-empty room as if it were a full stadium. She sang and danced, pranced and swiveled. Her hair was pulled up tight into a high ponytail that she swung around to accent her moves.

"I wonder if she goes to a chiropractor for all of that neck swinging and snapping," Olive mused.

"At minimum, I'll bet she goes home with a headache after each show," I said.

We munched on our salads and sandwiches, pivoting our gaze from the ocean to Donna. Off at the dark end of the bar, a man sat and sipped his drink. Before his glass was empty, the bartender refilled it. The man didn't watch or seem to listen to Donna, which would be difficult with the amplifiers and her movements. She engaged her scant audience by going near their tables, patting the arms of men and women as she sang. She kept an eye on the man at the bar. I imagine she was gauging how she could hook and reel him in.

Donna sang one of the songs Isabelle Simone had sung the other night. That felt weird. The man at the bar glared at her and looked back down at the bar, shaking his head slowly. That momentary eye contact was all Donna seemed to need. I could only see part of his face but, to me it was a warning kind of look. Donna must have seen it differently.

"Ladies and gentlemen, we have a surprise guest with us this afternoon. Mr. Bertrand D'Lamore is attempting to keep to himself at the far end of the bar. Do you see him? Hello, Bertrand!" She fluttered her fingers in a wave to him. Getting no response, Donna turned to the few guests.

"Now I ask you, ladies and gentlemen, does anyone go out to a casino and expect not to be seen? No, of course not. Bertrand, my love, won't you sing with me?" She walked toward him.

The time it took Bertrand to drain his glass, pull money out of his pocket, and toss several bills onto the bar was all Donna needed to close in on him. She slid her satin-covered body up against Bertrand's and had one hand stroking his arm. He stood ramrod straight, head held high, and looked straight ahead.

Donna motioned to the barkeep for a drink for Bertrand as she sang "Let Me Entertain You" while crawling her fingers up and down

Bertrand's arm. She had Bertrand in hand, and she wasn't letting him get away.

"Bertrand, we have known one another for many years, dancing and singing together all over the island. We have laughed together and, how shall I say it for our guests, comforted each other through difficult times when no one else would, haven't we, Bertrand?" Donna laid her head against his chest.

Bertrand tensed his body as if an electric current went through it, so intense, it pushed Donna away from him. Bertrand grabbed Donna by the arm this time and pulled her very close as he lowered his head to her ear, said something, and stormed out of the casino lounge. Donna looked broken. There she stood, alone, in the middle of the dance floor. We just sat there to see what she would do next.

She stared at the floor for a few seconds and when her head snapped back upright, Performance Donna was back. "Well, ladies and gentleman, let's get this party started." She began singing a quick-paced, energized song about being on the beach, drinking beer, and having fun. Donna didn't say another word about the scene she had created with Bertrand.

We finished eating and walked through the restaurant and casino on our way out. Coco said, "Well, that was a bit more theater than I expected at a casino. I planned for the slot machines to be the highlight of my day, but whatever that was between Mr. D'Lamore and Donna was something else. At first, I thought he was going to give in and let her have her way with him because, let's face it, most men would. But oh no. He went with the more demur murmur in her ear and then strode out in righteous anger."

Olive added, "I wonder what he said to her. It didn't look like a thank-you—it looked more like a threat."

"Whatever it was," I said, "it stopped her in her tracks and seemed to completely disarm her, but just for a second, didn't it? When her head came back up, her eyes were steely but her performance was back on."

We walked across a parking lot and saw that detective lady talking to someone at their car. Oh, she was talking with Bertrand. That's what I started to call him, as if we knew each other and were on a first-name basis. They finished their conversation, and the detective caught us watching them. I waved in greeting, and she headed over to us holding her notepad in one hand.

"Great," said Brie, "see how she still has her notepad out? She's coming to ask questions. Can you please remember that we are tourists here and have no part in her investigation? We are in a foreign country and she is a police officer. Don't push it!"

Coco reached out a welcoming hand to the officer, who wasn't smiling. Coco, always good at socializing and warming up to strangers, started chatting about the beautiful weather and her enrollment in the medical conference.

The officer waited for a break in Coco's spiel. "I saw the four of you the night of the murder and you, Ms. V. Ahern, were seen with the costumes. Then again, I saw you in Phillipsburg at the café talking with Dru. And then again in the bookstore that belongs to Isabelle's aunt. Now this afternoon, I see you at the casino where there is an altercation between Ms. Fleur and Mr. D'Lamore."

"Those do seem to be a lot of coincidences once you point them all out," Olive agreed.

I read her name tag and smiled. Detective Pamela Poissonier didn't smile back. "No, I am investigating a death, which appears to be murder, and everywhere I look, I find the four of you. What is your relation to this investigation?"

"Us?" I said. "None. We have no relationship to this death."

"I am here for a medical conference on Saba Island," Coco stated with great dignity.

"I'm just here to have fun when Coco isn't at her conference. We travel together sometimes," Olive added.

"Brie and I have been to Saint Martin several times so we arranged to be here when my sister," I slid my eyes toward Olive, "would be here so we could all have fun together. It has been interesting that wherever we go, we meet someone or overhear something about the murder."

By now, the sun was starting to bake us onto the asphalt parking lot and sweat was running down our temples. Detective Poissonier gave no indication of discomfort or of moving. I really wanted to help, so I told her everything we had learned. From the server at breakfast, to the conversation with Dru, to what we heard in the bookstore, to the scene in the casino.

"I was wondering if the woman in the bookstore was Isabelle's mother when she talked about the quality of meats she expected for such an important funeral celebration." I glanced over at my sister and winked. I came back to the detective. "It seems that Bertrand and Isabelle loved each other but couldn't be together for some reason. Dru seemed to be in love with Isabelle, and from what we just saw, Donna seems to be in love with Bertrand. Does it seem that way to you, Detective?"

"I am not at liberty to discuss this investigation with tourists, or anyone, for that matter. I suggest you talk about our fine weather, food, and swimming. Asking questions about an ongoing investigation, however exciting to you, could become problematic if you were seen as an impediment to this investigation. Do I make myself clear?"

Brie spoke. "Very clear, Detective. The sisters are always in search of new soup recipes for a pizzeria back in Maine. We will focus on tasting as many delicious foods as possible in the time we are here. You probably won't see us again, unless it is in a restaurant by the ocean."

"But," I clarified, "Coco is at the medical conference and the body is there, so we may hear something from Coco. And we can't help if everywhere we've gone so far has employed someone from the other night. Brie works in politics at the local and state levels, so what if she takes a tour of the desalination plant and runs into Bertrand? She can't be rude."

Brie sighed. The detective sighed. I held my breath as I realized what I'd just said. Coco and Olive were starting to quiver. Whatever happened next would be due to their fear. They were either going to burst out laughing or wet their pants and cry. They each took a couple steps backward to put some space between them and us. The detective saw them move, saw their shoulders shaking. When she looked at their faces, Olive's and Coco's eyes got large with fright. They looked like deer caught in headlights. Detective Poissonier sighed again and looked from me to Brie. She said something to Brie in French, touched the brim of her cap, turned, and walked to her cruiser.

"What did she say to you, Brie?" Olive asked.

"She wished me good luck at keeping you three from endangering yourselves or getting in the way of this investigation. You have to stop asking questions," Brie attempted to scold us.

"Well," I said, "we start by genuinely expressing our condolences to people who were here on Friday night and before we know it, they're giving us more information."

"Wait a minute," said Brie, "before you know it? Before the person knows it, you've gained their trust and they're answering your questions. Do you think they would give the officer as much information?"

"Well, I'm just being curious and polite," I nattered back.

While we continued crossing the searing parking lot, we saw the officer in her cruiser, writing madly in her notebook.

"Keep walking, eyes forward, and don't say a word," Brie said.

It was time for an afternoon swim.

What a luxurious swim it was. I could have floated all the way to China and still been happy. I swam overhand. I swam backstroke. I swam a couple of twirl-arounds but mostly floated. It was fun to breathe deeply and feel my lungs expand and make me more buoyant. Letting it out and sinking—first my butt, then my feet—was playful.

Brie got in her beach walk. She walked ankle-deep in the water, binoculars in hand in case she spotted a bird.

Olive doesn't really like getting wet. With her beach cover-up and hat on, she stood in the water at shin depth. As the sand went out from under her, she kept moving, looking like she was marching in place. Coco went between the two of us. She imagined herself an Olympic swimmer. She splashed her way out to me. We looked at each other underwater, then waved and screamed something so the other could try to understand what was shouted—a wacky version of telephone tag. Then she swam back to Olive and did handstands in the water to make Olive laugh. Also to splash her, but it was all in fun.

Completely stretched out from the water and pooped out from the casino and walking, we headed to the showers. Fresh clothing and ice-cold tea was invigorating. We brought our food together in our apartment and ate dinner on the balcony. We lingered through sunset and then went inside.

We are news-watching people, so Brie put the TV on to catch the local news. It was in French, so Olive, Coco, and I made up what we thought the story was. Brie was practicing her compassionate kindness as she listened.

I dished out ice cream and brought the bowls into the living room. "So what's going on now? Did I just hear Isabelle Simone's name?"

Brie's arms went out straight from her sides. Kind of like the umpire signaling "safe" to a runner. The three of us took it to mean "shut up." She listened while we watched. The news reporter was sitting in the studio and saying something in French with a serious look on his face. When he stopped, there was a second or two and they rolled some footage. It was Detective Poissonier in the casino parking lot this afternoon. It showed her talking with Bertrand D'Lamore. And then…

"Oh my God!" I said.

"You three!" Brie charged.

"We're gonna be famous!" Olive sang out.

There we were, on the island evening news. Waving like old high school friends to Bertrand and the detective. There was a quick camera switch back to the detective and her unhappy face as she straightened up from Bertrand's car. Brie interpreted that the reporter labeled us as tourists who waved because we had probably noticed the news crew van and camera. That didn't even make sense.

"Detective Poissonier is going to be so mad at us!" I said.

"It isn't our fault the camera couldn't resist us," Coco quipped.

"Wait," Brie broke in. "He's saying that we were interviewed because we had been in the casino when Bertrand had an altercation with the performer, Donna Fleur."

"So we're material witnesses?" I didn't know what made a person a material witness as opposed to an immaterial one, but I thought that sounded more important than just being people in a crowd.

Brie went and poured some wine. When she looked at me and raised the bottle, I nodded in assent. Olive and Coco took the cue and left, chattering about the possibilities for who would play them in the movie.

Back out on the balcony, looking out into the warm darkness, Brie let out a low chuckle.

"What?"

She said, "You and your sister are something. This is serious stuff that is happening here, but you two, egged on by Coco, are so darned funny, I can't help but laugh."

"Oh, honey." I put an arm around her. "Laugh is what my family does. You don't want to be in the car with us during a funeral procession. We put ourselves into hysterical nervous laughter. And that's before we break out the hidden snacks."

"Snacks? In a funeral procession? Why am I not surprised? My grandmother Quirion would smack me into the next week for a stunt like that. The sacrilege of it would have me in Hail Marys' for a month."

"Well," I patted her back and led her inside, "your grandmother can watch all of this from above and be glad that she was related to you and not me."

We rinsed out the wine glasses, brushed our teeth, and settled in for a long summer's sleep.

Chapter Eleven

Coco had left on the water shuttle to Saba by the time Brie and I met Olive after breakfast. We went to the Butterfly Farm, one of the island's ecotourism sites. Our goal for lunch was Loterie Farm, known for its tapas and other well-presented, delicious food.

Inside the butterfly-netted ceilings and walls, Brie had her identification book out and was conversing in French with one of the scientists. Olive and I were transported by the fairylike quality of the place. The largest butterflies I had ever seen would alight on our shoulders or the tops of our heads. They must have been shy because they never sat still quite long enough for me to take a photo. While looking at a nearby flower, I stumbled upon the tiniest ones, no larger than my thumbnail.

The blue morpho, with its brown outline and white dots trimming the aqua wings, was exciting and calming at the same time. It was exciting to see such intricate and detailed beauty so close. Gazing at the creature silently resting on a leaf with wings splayed wide sent a feeling of calm right through me. It was a unique experience. If I hadn't had sweat dripping down and off my nose and chin, I could have gazed at it for a long time. I purchased my first trip-gift for myself: a lighter-than-air porcelain replica as a Christmas ornament.

We had dutifully sipped from our lukewarm water bottles all morning and were ready for something cold and sweet when we arrived up the mountain at Loterie Farm. The covered restaurant deck was luxurious; white overstuffed sofas against the perimeter railing kept everyone safe. Those outside walls were merely curtains beyond the railing. They could be closed during rain and tied back with golden ropes otherwise. Low tables were used for holding drinks and small dishes. People were here during the busy times to see and be seen. This was a sophistication level higher than our normal, and we enjoyed being among the beautiful people.

We all agreed to forego the walking path and zip line. We left those to the families and younger couples. Sitting on the deck, we could look 180 degrees over the forest. It was verdant and lush. The textures from different plants, the cloudless robin's-egg-blue sky all wrapped up in eighty-five-degree weather was my idea of paradise. I leaned back into the plush pillow cushion and spread one arm over the back thinking I looked like a celebrity or an actress in a movie. Gosh, it was terrific.

I decided on a mimosa with freshly squeezed orange juice. Brie had chilled red sangria, and Olive had a glass of water with kiwi slices. Small plates of assorted olives, bruschetta with oil and herbs, a hot cup of soup made with kale, corn, bok choy, and garbanzo beans seasoned heartily in a vegetable broth were delish. Another small plate of grilled shrimp added heft. The cold soup—caramelized pineapple with pecans, peas, and peaches with a dollop of sour cream on top—was so unusual, we all marveled over it.

Whoever thought to caramelize a pineapple should never have to work again. Genius. A bit of work but still amazing. Turning an already sweet fruit into a more robust, almost heady bit of sweetness was brilliant. Who has the time and creativity to think of these things? What else could we caramelize? I thought it was just onions. The fruits and vegetable were pureed, but there were enough pineapple bits to lend a nice texture. The soup was presented with a layer of chopped pecans placed on top. Our waiter told us this was one recipe he could use to get his son to eat a vegetable.

The wait staff pleasantly refilled our water bottles and we walked the gardens until the relentless sun became too much. We left for our home away from home.

"Well," said Brie, "it has been nice to have a quiet day."

"It's not over," Olive said. "We still have dinner with Coco. You never know what can happen."

Maneuvering the rental over the mountainous roads required all of my attention. Driving had my attention while Olive and Brie's conversation drifted through me.

"Wait! What's that?" I said. A big sign with "Saint Gerolamo Emiliani Orphanage of Saint Martin" was posted on the front lawn next to a long driveway that led up to an old but nice adobe home. Behind it were newer two-story buildings. I pulled in rather sharply.

"Hey," yelled Brie, "what are you doing? We can't just go in here!"

I put the car into park. "Well, what are they going to do, arrest me for being lost, for being curious, for turning around in their driveway? We aren't doing anything illegal. We'll just drive up and see what we see."

"So much for my quiet day," Brie muttered.

I had pulled up in front of the main house. At least two of us were craning our necks as Mr. Tipo stepped out and came to my window looking kind. I rolled it down.

"Good afternoon, madams. You are either generous soon-to-be benefactors of our orphanage or you are lost on your way down the mountain from Loterie Farm."

"Actually," I said, "we are both. We were at the fundraiser last Friday at the resort." Was that a slight wince in his eyes? "We are already benefactors and are on our way back from a lovely lunch. We saw your sign and thought we would stop in to see what we might see."

I continued, "I used to teach in special education, and my sister, Olive, works in elementary schools teaching a personal body safety program for our youngest students. They learn how to keep themselves safe from predators and what to do if someone violates their trust. And Brie works in politics, both federal and local, so we each have different interests in how this wonderful island takes care of its most vulnerable." It was all true but as I said it, I thought it sounded like a fib.

"You sound as though you share our determined compassion for children. Why don't you step out of your vehicle? I'll get someone to give you a brief tour."

An old woman with very curly gray hair pulled into a high bun came by just at that time.

"Esther, would you be so kind as to show these ladies around? They are kindred spirits."

Esther was just over five feet tall and slightly stooped, but her voice, low and smooth, made her sound stronger than she appeared.

"Of course, Mr. Tipo," she said. "Let's get you out of the sun and humidity. Each building is air-conditioned or has ceiling fans."

We entered the homelike building. "Please sign our Guest Register so we have a record of your visit," Esther guided us to a reception desk. "There are connecting tunnels between buildings, so we are spared being out in the heat or tropical rains."

"Olive," I commented, "they're just like the tunnels at the Tewksbury State Hospital." Turning to our tour guide, "Miss Esther, where Olive and I grew up, we have a state hospital and some children lived there who were wards of the state, but it is a hospital for all kinds of people with problems. The buildings were connected by tunnels. Those tunnels kept people out of the cold and snow. In Massachusetts, we don't have tropical heat like you do here."

"Thankfully," Esther continued, "we are on the mountain and tunnels are possible. Let's go top to bottom and back up again." She led us up a flight of stairs to the far right of the lobby.

On the second floor, we came into an open lobby with double doors leading into the building's interior. "The second floor is used as our auditorium. Let's go in."

There was a stage on the far end of the room. Another set of glass double doors led out onto the covered porch. About a dozen kids of all ages were stretching, reviewing dance steps, or sitting on the floor waiting to be told what to do. There were moveable ballet barres and a row of mirrors that looked as though they were moveable, too.

"Oh!" Esther's voice went into a raspy whisper. "Here is our Donna rehearsing with some of the children. We will be quiet and try not to disturb them," Esther explained.

We jumped as Donna barked, "Too late!"

It wasn't hard to overhear Donna harshly confronting an adolescent girl who had just slipped into the rehearsal hall, obviously late. That girl, with her glitter eye shadow and thick eyeliner, was having none of it. The other girls wore earth-tone T-shirts and tie-around-the-waist ruffled skirts over their shorts with graying, scuffed ballet slippers. This girl wore a skintight, teal crop top with spaghetti straps. Her deep-purple cropped yoga pants were also skintight, and she had slightly tattered but brilliantly white slippers.

"Olive," I whispered, "do you think she uses white shoe polish on her slippers like we used to do with our Keds?"

"Esperanza," Donna continued, "do you think you can just walk into a place, start singing and dancing, and people will throw their money at you? You don't think you need to practice or be on time or respect your teacher?"

"Whatever," said Esperanza with curled lip.

Donna looked over at us. She caught Esther's measured gaze.

Olive murmured, "I'm so glad my kids are through this phase."

Donna took a deep breath and continued, this time with a milder tone. "Oh, my young friend, let me tell you what I have learned. First, you become what the audience wants to see and hear. Make them believe that you exist purely for their enjoyment. Be humble. Your reason for being in their presence is to make them feel good. They have to want to see and hear you again and again before you can make changes that let you make your mark, not before."

We stood still, mesmerized by Donna's lecture. Plus, we were kind of afraid to interrupt again by moving to leave.

"I purposely keep you in the younger girls' costumes with ruffles. You feel ready for the women's costumes? You think your developing bosoms and cleavage under a low-cut blouse will bring you what you want? You want to flip your skirts in that flirtatious way we mature women do? You plan to catch the eye of men and think that will bring you power and wealth? Listen to me." Donna put a hand on each of Esperanza's shoulders. "If you want to remain in the chorus line, then jump into that costume, but you will be forfeiting a great opportunity."

Olive muttered, "Here comes an eye roll. These years are torture for everyone."

"Wear the younger girls' costume," Donna continued.

Esperanza, as if on cue, rolled her eyes away from Donna.

Donna persevered. "Let the blouse get just a little tight and the skirt a bit short. Show that you are outgrowing your childhood. That look catches the wealthy women's eyes. They recognize this uncomfortable stage in themselves. Men control the money. Women, smart women, control the men."

Olive sputtered but whispered, "Don't tell her that! Esperanza just needs a good cup of tea, someone to talk with, and maybe some 5-HTP."

Brie just looked at Olive and went back to the scene unfolding before us.

"And when you are onstage smiling," Donna went on, "you catch the eye of one of these women and she makes the smallest nod to let you know she sees you and is rooting for you. And as you twirl away, your reply smile shows an extra glow for her. And when you introduce yourself at curtain call, you look directly at her and introduce yourself only to her. Your reward comes when she smiles back with the same glow you gave her."

Esperanza tapped her toe on the floor and crossed her arms.

Donna continued, "I see your impatience with this but I tell you—it works. Esperanza, now is the time to build your bridge out of this life, out of this orphanage, out of this identity that you have created about yourself and what those idiots at school have told you for years. Espie, you are so much more than this place and those fools. You will need to be ready to turn eighteen when all of these supports around you fall. You start now building the supports for the day you leave here."

"Are we dancing today or just listening?" one boy asked with a smirk. "Because I have some bridges of my own to build."

"Oh, Otto," said Donna, "you should take heed of this information as well. You think you're going to walk out of here at eighteen and a good job will be waiting for you? I'll get to you later." Donna turned back to Esperanza, who was biting a hangnail off one finger.

"So, Espie, you have made contact and you are back here, waiting. Weeks later, Mr. Tipo might come to rehearsal to read a letter of appreciation for our performance from the woman's husband that mentions the special joy Esperanza brought his wife. And he has included a generous check."

Esperanza's eyes lit up wide and hopeful.

"Oh! You think it is for you? No, no. It is for our future performances."

Esperanza's eyes steeled themselves from yet another disappointment.

Donna went on, "You still think you haven't gotten anything out of this? Remember, you have been practicing every day since then. You are even better than when you impressed this woman. Because of your appeal and smile, you are moved into the front line of the chorus and you keep catching the eyes of wealthy women who see themselves in you. Who get their wealthy husbands to write checks. Now what do you do? You write thank-you cards, not to the men, but to the wives. And you tell each of them your dreams. Yes, you tell them. And you write of your insecurities around being able to fit into society outside the orphanage walls when you turn eighteen. You write to each woman."

Esperanza was leaning forward, listening.

"One day," Donna went on, "one of them will invite you to lunch with her in Marigot. And if she likes you, if she feels safe with you."

Esperanza's eyes grew wide.

"Yes, safe. She cannot think for an instant that your blossoming beauty might become a threat to her standing with her wealthy husband. We don't know how this woman became this wealthy man's wife and what she has become in order to remain in his good graces and wealth. If she feels safe, she may become a benefactor. And then you may get special dance and voice lessons, tutors in difficult school subjects, invitations to restaurants you only see on television. You may have new clothes and a haircut at a fancy salon, not Esther's crooked blunt cuts."

Donna held the girl's gaze. "If you are as bright and cunning as we both know you can be, you will take your opportunities as they present themselves. Even this awkward, restless fourteen-year-old part. Turn your discomfort into a step toward fulfilling your dreams. Espie, every woman, every woman feels like you are feeling now. Make it work for you. Don't try to skip over it. Work it. Our wealthy sisters can show you options for your life and help you get there."

Esperanza gaped at Donna.

"Adulthood will come soon enough, my dove—use this time wisely to get ready." Donna gave Esperanza a knowing look and turned toward the rest of the group. "As for the rest of us, let's sing our warm-up songs! Gather round, into position."

I finally took a breath. I hadn't been aware that I'd held it for most of this handing-of-the-baton lecture. "Holy mackinoly, nobody taught us those lessons in public school. Maybe some girls learned to play by those rules, but I sure didn't. Just think about how this girl sees the world and her place in it. At least she's getting some mentoring from a woman she views as a success. Geez, it brings a whole new level of meaning to aspirations."

Off to one side of the room, a petite girl caught my eye. She had long brown hair, large brown eyes with lashes that wouldn't quit, and a glow to her light-brown skin. She was standing quietly, watching and listening to the argument turned lecture. She looked to be about eight years old. Esther followed my gaze and mentioned, "That is Helder. She is a lovely child. No bother at all, ever. Like her name, she is bright."

"She's learning to be invisible," I said.

"Ah, you know something about not bringing on the attention of others," Esther observed.

I answered, "I've been flying below the radar all my life. Helder won't be the cause of a lecture or scolding. She'll not only learn what not to do, to avoid such reprimands, but she'll also learn the lesson from this lecture as well. Double the learning, lessen the strife."

Esther patted my shoulder and moved over to Olive and Brie, who were looking at the photographs lining the back wall of the hall. "Our graduates. There is our Donna. Many times performing with Isabelle Simone, may she rest in peace. Isabelle was brought up to give to the needy, to make their day lighter if she could. She and Donna got along well. Isabelle was kind to her in school, and Donna's confidence grew as a result. She practiced dances and songs until she could perform exactly like in the movies or on MTV. That is how she was chosen to work in Isabelle's dance troupe."

Brie mentioned, "They look a bit alike, right next to each other in that photo, don't they?"

Olive and I nodded.

Esther led us out the rear single door from the auditorium and down different stairs than we had come up. "We have had an anonymous benefactor funding a dance teacher for many years. That teacher must have seen the potential in Donna because she often took special interest and made extra time with her. Whenever there were new shoes to hand out, one pair always seemed fit Donna perfectly."

Back on the first floor were three offices. The first one was damaged with black scorch marks and police tape keeping people away.

"This was our Records Room. Please excuse the mess. It is where the fire broke out. We were to have all the records scanned and kept safe forever, but now we have far fewer to save."

She turned from the room back to us. "We keep an eye on the room as much as we can. There is always a child or two trying to snoop around, but those records are sealed, just as in your United States. People who give their children away do not do it lightly. It is never easy for anyone involved. Children often ask about their parents. We tell them the facts as we know them."

"Did Donna ask about her birth family?" I asked.

"Oh yes. We told Donna that her mother was a beautiful Haitian woman. We didn't have information in our records about her father," she said, shaking her head, "Donna made up stories about who he might be and how she came to be an orphan. Many children do. She suffered the typical adolescent rages and would scream that her father threw her away, didn't want her, treated her like trash." Again, the slow shaking head.

"She has never taken to the idea that something bad may have happened to her father, that perhaps he was killed before she was born or that he wanted and loved her but simply could not be a single father. Records that she so desperately wanted to see were some of those destroyed. Now she'll never have the meager facts that we had."

We continued down yet another flight of stairs into the basement where the tunnels started. Olive, Brie, and I were moving slowly and carefully. Esther moved nimbly on these steep and narrow stairs.

Brie said, "My knees are getting sore."

After walking down an underground hallway, we turned right and climbed up stairs into a large dining room in one of the new buildings. We sat for iced tea and cookies. Esther gave each of us a small plastic bag with a frozen sponge in it. Brie rubbed hers on her knees. So did Esther. Olive and I used ours on our necks and wrists to cool down. Just walking was costly in this weather.

"Coming downstairs was painful enough, but going up isn't any easier," Brie said on our way back. "I'll be ready for a couple of aspirin from our travel medical bag when we get back to the car."

Olive suggested, "And maybe rub some Arnica on your knees."

I ignored both of them, keeping my focus on Esther's story. Walking out to the car, I asked, "Does Donna know her real and full name now? She is in her twenties. No longer under the orphanage's restrictions? Does she have a right to information?"

"Oh yes," Esther said. "When she turned eighteen, we told Donna her full name. She continued asking about her records and details of her birth. We showed her the certificate of birth. It gave her mother's surname. It documented that the father was not present. The only other documents were the notes from the delivering midwife, all medical numbers and any notes of interest at the time. Donna ignored those. Digging up the past is painful. Since the fire, her questioning has stopped."

Esther continued, "We don't speak of parents and how a child becomes an orphan. Life is difficult enough just living day to day with the uncertainty, shame, and doubts, as you can imagine. Our children attend the local public schools, and children as well as adults can be cruel in what they say and in how they accept and incorporate them into their school community. Our children face lives of not belonging, of not feeling wanted. This is where they are safe, and our job is to make them ready to enter the world at age eighteen."

"Well," I said, "we have taken up enough of your time, Esther. Thank you for the tour and refreshments. I've had enough for one day and am ready for a good swim. Whether that will come before or after a nap is yet to be decided." After more thanks and good wishes, we drove away.

Brie stretched out in the back seat so she could nap. Olive and I traded ideas back and forth the whole way back to the Peacock. Olive offered up a class issue. "What if the Haitian mother was pregnant by a wealthy, upper-class, lighter-skinned man? Of course a wealthy man of any color couldn't have an affair or, heaven forbid in this culture, actually love a darker-skinned and lower-leveled woman. Like that never happens. I'll bet there are more than a few kids in that orphanage under those circumstances. But no one talks about it. Those children didn't ask to be born, but they pay the price." She was spitting by now. "So there may be some wealthy guy out there with not one bit of responsibility for his child. His love child."

I mused, "I wonder if he knows about Donna. If the mother never had a man around when the midwife came to see her and she was alone during the delivery, who was this guy? If the mother said the father's name, can you imagine someone from the orphanage or midwifery agency going to him and telling him that his child was born and oh, by the way, the mother died right after birth? Would a paternity test be done? If not, he could just deny the whole thing and go merrily along with his life."

"I hope his guilt eats away at him," Olive hissed.

"Donna is in her twenties now. If the father had any guilt, don't you think he would have shown it somehow by now?" I asked. "Poor Donna. Can you imagine how many dreadful stories she's made up in her mind about her family? All she knows is that she's half Haitian. Or does she just assume both parents were Haitian? What is it like not to know your family tree? And how does she feel now that she's aged out of the orphanage? No wonder she still goes back to help. It's the only home she knows."

"That can be crazy-making," said Olive. "Working with those kids is probably healing for Donna. She gets to be caring and nurturing to other children. Maybe some of that transfers back to nurturing herself. Can you imagine if she ever found out that she has a father walking around this island with tons of money and he knows about her but never did a darned thing?"

"Now that would be crazy-making," I said. "How could a heart withstand that?"

We drove on, appreciating our own families and the air conditioning in the rental car. We fiddled with the radio and found a music station that sounded festive. Brie was stretched out across the back seat. We could hear her foot tapping the door to the beat. I looked in the rearview mirror at her. "Good afternoon, Sunshine. Did you have a nice nap?"

"Oh sure, with you two analyzing different possibilities of the birth of a local entertainer? I hate to tell you, but Donna is doing fine. She doesn't need your sympathy or interference. Let's talk about the butterflies or the food from today. Olive, what was your favorite part?"

Olive and I glanced at each other and smiled. "Let's see," Olive thought aloud, "my favorite part was a teeny butterfly that was pinky-purplish. It was so tiny and light. Then I think I liked the hot soup more than the cold pineapple one. Any time I have cold fruit, I think of tossing it into a blender with some yogurt and making a smoothie."

I chimed in, "I don't know. Caramelizing a pineapple? That was great. It takes some of the bite out of it and makes it so sweet! That was dessert by itself. I don't know how cold soup would go over in central Maine. Maybe in the summertime, all two weeks of it. Brie, you enjoy a good gazpacho now and then. Do you think a cold soup would sell?"

Brie considered the concept. "Well, maybe as a special on those high-traffic weekends like the college graduations and maybe when families from out of state are dropping off and picking their kids up from camp."

Olive said, "I'll need to make some and see if it freezes well, if at all."

After a few minutes of quiet, Olive said, "I can't wait to hear what Coco learned at the conference today. We should be getting back right around the time she gets back from Saba."

Brie muttered from the back, "So much for getting these two off the hunt in this murder."

Chapter Twelve

As we walked toward the elevators, we saw Coco gliding through the lobby carrying a towel. She was in her bright-red flowered swimsuit and glittery red flip-flops. It's about time a size twenty-two looked so stylish.

"Coco, what is that flowery thing in your hand?" Olive asked.

"It's my bathing cap, isn't it great?" she said. "I don't plan on wearing it, but I loved it in the store so I got it. Won't it look cute on my towel while I'm in the water doing my water ballet? Come join me when you're ready!"

We agreed and appreciated Coco's sheer joy and lack of inhibition as we stepped into the elevator. We changed into bathing suits. I grabbed my bag already packed with hat, sunscreen, book, floating noodle, and towel. Brie grabbed only her hat and book while Olive tossed all of her gear into her towel and carried it like a vagabond's knapsack.

Down on the beach, Brie settled and stretched into a lounge chair. She was mewling. Olive and I took our noodles and joined Coco in the water. We latched onto one another's noodles with one hand so we were our own triangular barge of floating women. The water felt so good! The waves lulled and splashed us around, once in a while bumping us into other groups of people. Three women in their wide-brimmed sunhats had noodles behind their backs and under their arms. They each had a cold drink in one hand and tried holding on to one another as waves broke on them. They didn't think to move five feet out to get beyond those breaking waves on the shore. They were laughing hysterically. Everyone was happy and laughing.

Between crashes, we took turns attempting handstands in the water. We made a hysterical spectacle of ourselves with unsynchronized swimming. Noodles behind our necks, holding them with outstretched hands. Together, we kicked three times and moved backward, lifting our left legs high into the sky and floating wherever the water took us. It is hard to be graceful when you're laughing out loud in the ocean, especially when a wave breaks over you and you're coughing out seawater and squeezing your eyes shut. We wore ourselves out and called time-out for something to eat.

Coco said, "Next time, let's get those mermaid tails you see kids wearing!"

Olive doubled over at the mental picture of us. "Can you imagine trying to slither from the blanket into the surf? How do you spell *no way?!*"

We shook our wet hair all over Brie, who really liked it, as you can imagine. Salt, water, and a bit of sand tumbling down onto her brought out a yelp and a cuss word or two before she remembered where she was and her better manners.

"Hey," I said, "you can't be the only one dry and pristine."

"Why the heck not? I wasn't a circus act in the water. I was minding my own business, ready to call 911 if one of you got a cramp in your leg and needed to be extricated from the surf," she laughed. "You three could be heard all the way up here on the beach over those squealing kids with their little foam surfboards. I don't know which laughter I enjoyed more, yours as relaxed and carefree adults or the kids, who find joy so easily." She swept her arm out and around. "This is great. But now that you're out of the water, why don't you hose yourselves down in the outdoor showers and we'll move over to the patio for some dinner?"

Olive, Coco, and I quickly showered off the bulk of the salt and sand and rejoined Brie, who was watching the airplanes land and take off across the bay.

The four of us walked over to the outdoor restaurant, getting a table with sun and shade. We noted every hue of blue, from the near-black of some of the boulders in the seawall to the light aqua bleeding out to dirty white when the water became surf. The mild breeze from the water and a temperature in the mid-eighties made for another perfect moment.

Brie asked, "So Coco, how was your conference today? Did you learn any new natural treatments?"

"Actually, I did," Coco began. "Brie, you're a flower person. You probably already know this, but it was news to me. We learned that people have used the belladonna plant, watered down, of course, for centuries in everything from medicines for sedation and seizure control to eye drops so women could dilate their pupils and look more seductive."

"Of course women did that," snarled Olive. "So stupid." She shook her head.

Coco continued, "The belladonna flower is beautiful, but it can also kill you. During the autopsy, doctors found the flower's poison, atropine, in Isabelle's bloodstream. Can you imagine?"

An all businesslike waitress came over and took drink orders while handing out menus. We all ordered water to start.

Olive asked, "Did she die from smelling it?"

"No, it can kill by contact as well as by getting into the bloodstream."

We each sat with that until our waitress came back with the water, explaining the specials as she placed the glasses on the table. "Tonight we have papayas in our specials to serve you. We have a refreshing cold drink that has papaya, pineapple, and ginger. Next, we have a cold soup with pineapple, papaya, lemons, limes, and a tangy pomegranate juice—very good on an evening such as this. We also have shrimp salad with a baguette and cheese. And we have a whitefish grilled with capers, lemon, and island herbs."

Olive jumped on the beverage. "I'll try the drink, please. And I'll have the whitefish special."

Coco ordered a Corona and a cheeseburger. Brie ordered red wine with a cup of the soup and the baguette with a salad. I had a cold chardonnay with something from the regular menu: quinoa salad with herbed grilled shrimp. The waitress walked away to the next table to take their orders.

"So she held the flower and died? What's the length of time from contact to death? She didn't have any flowers during the show," I said.

"The poison got into her bloodstream somehow, but here's the weirdness of it."

"Oh," chimed in Brie, "now it gets weird? I can't wait to hear this."

Coco continued, "The bra cups of Isabelle's costume had been dusted with the dried and crushed berries. It's as though someone took a flour sifter and spread the dust all over the inside of her top. As Isabelle sweat during the performance, it would have transferred into her system."

"Ugh!" said Olive, putting her hand to her chest. "I can tell you how it got into her system. She either drank it from that woman's glass of water or, more than likely, it was from the cut on her breast from Dru and that gross and dirty cash. And you!" She pointed toward me. "You had that costume in your hands! Did you get any on you?" I blew her off with a dismissive hand gesture.

She turned to Coco. "How deadly is this dust? Isabelle was only sweating a little."

"Remember that we noticed Isabelle wasn't sweating nearly as much as the other performers? We joked about where she might conceal ice packs in that scanty costume. She must have already been getting sick."

Our waitress was still at the other table. Island time, I thought. Quickly reprimanding myself that I should take a lesson, I sat back in my chair, something I don't normally do.

"Oh my gosh, Olive, that's great that you remembered that! So the atropine from the belladonna plant seeped into her system and reduced her sweating during the performance," Coco said.

"And remember that she said her wooziness must have been jet lag? I wonder if that was part of the poisoning, too," I added. "And, and, wait for it, remember when Bertrand made that smarmy remark about how Isabelle's heart was racing and her face was flushed when she was in his arms? What about that, Coco?"

"All symptoms of the poisoning. I'll bring these observations back to the conference. It may help. Okay, back to the money," Coco went on, "if that hadn't happened, Isabelle would have gotten really sick but it probably wouldn't have killed her. The open cut let the poison go directly into her bloodstream. The dust started making her ill, but the direct influx was enough to kill her."

"So whoever put the poison in her costume may not have wanted Isabelle dead, just ill," I said. "Why would someone do that?"

Brie said, "You gals are creating quite the wild story." She leaned closer to us across the table and said in hushed tones, "I just don't want to see Detective Poissonier again, so keep your fiction to yourselves, please. I don't want any trouble." There was a note of pleading in her voice. That Brie, how she hates trouble.

"Definitely," I said, sitting up straight, putting my clasped hands on the table like the good girl I could be.

Olive said, "Absolutely. My lips are sealed on this topic," as she gestured twisting a key to lock her lips closed.

Coco looked at Brie with a knowing grin. Olive and I would stop talking about it for now, but we would pick it up again as soon as we could.

Our food arrived. Brie's papaya, pineapple, and citrus soup, of which we each took a spoonful, was fun and refreshing.

Olive said, "It would make a good smoothie."

I took two tastes because, let's face it, I'm her wife, so I could. My shrimp snapped when I bit into it. It was so fresh and good. The quinoa salad under it had orange segments, some of the night's papaya, and a bit of oil and sea salt. Olive's whitefish was delicate and simple. She used a piece of Brie's baguette to sop up the oil and herbs left on her plate. Coco wondered where the island got its beef. Her burger was juicy and had a different texture than burgers at home. Her cheese was smoked Gouda, with a slice of onion, tomato, and a smattering of chopped lettuce. We oohed and aahed throughout the meal, sharing bites from one another's plates.

I didn't want to hold off on this fantastic story any longer. With an insincere apologetic look at Brie, I asked, "I don't think this is such a wild story, do you two? I think it all makes perfect sense. We need to see Detective Pamela."

"For what, Vidalia," Olive quipped, "to update her on our investigation? She would lock us up or at least escort us to the airport to get rid of us."

"Well, I just think we have information that she might not have. We're only trying to help," I justified however unsuccessfully.

"Vidalia," Brie started.

Uh-oh, I thought. She'd had enough of my curiosity and imagination. Brie was getting nervous.

"I didn't come here to bail you out of jail or to spend our time investigating a murder. Remember, we came here to relax, get warm, and eat good food. Let's just keep it to that, like Detective Poissonier strongly recommended. Your story is funny to listen to as you and your sister weave oddball bits into a seemingly convincing tale, but remember, you are not investigators. Neither of you has the qualifications to investigate a murder. I'll admit, your story is gripping, but that's all it is—a story."

Olive and I looked at Brie until she stopped talking. Our body language expressed our willingness to hear her out but that we weren't really going to heed her warning.

Brie took a last sip of water. "I'm heading up for a cooling shower and the news. Good night." Brie walked toward the hotel smiling, thinking she had ended our story-making.

Olive, Coco, and I finished our drinks. Olive said, "I really enjoyed this papaya, pineapple, ginger cooler. The heat from the fresh ginger was a perfect offset to the sweetness of the fruits. I'll have to remember this when I get home."

People were still in the water. Some were around the pool. The bar was surrounded by vacationers in bathing suits, shorts, or sundresses watching a soccer match on the television, cheering at times and jeering one another at other times. The blender drowned out the noise as it mixed ice with rum and various fruits. I noticed our waitress was talking on the phone—odd when it was so busy in the restaurant. We lingered as a cruise ship went back out to sea. There was a canopy set up closer to the water with a table for two arranged. A couple of torches had been lit, and an ice bucket held a bottle of what looked like champagne.

"Oh look," I said to Olive and Coco, "Looks like someone is about to become engaged."

Olive chimed in to the fabrication, "If this was a Hallmark movie, just as the proposal starts someone will break it up, or the real love of her life will see it and become despondent. He will do nothing about it, of course, and walk away with a broken heart, hopeless and helpless."

"That's good, Olive," Coco said. "Or a shark comes out of the water and bites off one of her legs."

Olive and I just looked at Coco.

"And then they have to fight to keep their love alive and strong." She put a hand to her chest and took a breath. "You know, like in those other movies where the couple has to overcome some adversity and then go on to save the exact same shark, an endangered shark that took her leg. Oh, I want Billy Joel to make the music for my movie."

"That's another way to go," said Olive. "I particularly like the fact that the shark is endangered. Nice touch."

Coco preened, "I just added that as I was talking." She bobbed her red, wavy hair. "You know, it's my creative genius."

"Hoo boy," I laughed, "by this point, poor Brie would be walking into the ocean, hoping a shark would take her. Our stories make her happily crazy. She doesn't think like this at all. Linear sequential, that's my girl. She says that we make her mind tired."

The night crowd was building. The music and noise that goes along with drinking were increasing so we called it a night. I was looking forward to sitting on our balcony, taking in the evening air.

In our apartment, a freshly showered Brie had turned on a French-speaking station for the news. I was at a loss, but different clips kept my attention. I tend to look at the background when I don't understand the language. There was footage of the funeral procession for Isabelle Simone. We could see the lady from the bookstore weeping. I understood *tante* in the caption.

Isabelle's mother and father stood stiffly together, holding hands. They were a wealthy-looking Brazilian couple whose only child had been killed. They were now comforting others in the receiving line. The newscaster was providing observations and identification of those in the line. We saw Donna. She was sobbing almost uncontrollably. When she got to Mr. Simone, she leaned her head against his chest and snuggled right up against him. He awkwardly raised his arms around her. And then he closed his eyes and they almost lingered there for a moment. The audio at the event went on, and we could hear what they said. Brie gave me a translation as they went.

Mr. Simone was saying, "Yes, I know that you two were close. She had many cherished friends and colleagues."

Donna stepped back, leveled her gaze at him, and said, "We were like sisters, weren't we, Monsieur Simone? Isabelle and I were so much like sisters."

Mr. Simone startled, put up his hands as if to defend himself, and took a step backward. His wife noticed something had happened and looked at her husband with a questioning and concerned look.

Then to his wife, he muttered, "The press warned us about some of the people who might show up here, but this is too much," and walked away from the line.

Donna was still in the camera frame, suddenly dry-eyed, watching Isabelle's father walk away.

Both of them were shaking.

"What the heck was that all about?" I said.

"Two very sad people misinterpreting what they hear and not being careful about what they say," said Brie.

"Maybe, but did you see how quickly Donna's eyes went from crying to dry and focused?" I asked.

"No, but I have no doubt you did, my story-making friend. I'll bet your sister saw it, too, if she was watching. Let's see how long it takes before she calls." She smiled, tapping her watch.

In the next instant, there was a knock at the door.

"Oh, you think you know us so well, don't you?" I called to Brie as I answered the knock. Olive was at the door.

"Ha!" Brie laughed. "Do I know you two or what?" She clapped her hands together and bent forward with laughter. She was so impressed with herself, she was tickled.

"I've brought two things to share. Hi, Brie, did you miss me?"

Brie attempted a scowl but her smile just distorted it, which made the moment even funnier.

"First," Olive continued, "I was looking through one of the magazines and saw this soup recipe and hope Brie will translate it for me because the picture looks mouthwatering." She handed the magazine to Brie, who got out a pen and pad of paper and sat at the dining room table.

"Oh, a hot soup with papaya. This does sound good," Brie said.

"Second, what was that on the news? Did you see how Donna went from nearly hysterical to clear-eyed the moment she got to Isabelle's father? What was that?"

"Brie translated for me. She and Isabelle were like sisters," I air quoted.

Olive snorted, "A lot of women are like sisters. More importantly, why did Mr. Simone react so strongly? He couldn't get away from Donna soon enough."

"I know," I said, "did you see that hug? There was something that happened and it didn't look like either one of them knew it was coming. I tell ya, there was something going on there."

Olive, known for knowing when to bring a conversation to a close, said, "Well, speculation can wait until tomorrow, right, Brie?"

Brie just looked at us and rolled her eyes knowing that even if we didn't talk about it, we would be thinking about what we saw and heard. "Did you two have boring childhoods? Did you sit around reading mystery books and making up your own stories?"

"No," I said, "we didn't have the pleasure of reading books growing up. Our parents didn't read books to us at night. None of that kind of thing. I didn't read for pleasure until after I got out of college, for the third time, actually. I never caught onto the idea that a book could whisk me away to another place or time. Maybe that's why I'm such a daydreamer. I've always made up movies in my head. Hmm, that's an interesting insight. I might reflect on that some more in my journal."

"Of course you will, you goober," said Olive as she walked toward the door. "Another insight for reflection. Good luck with that. Listen, I left Coco in such a rush I don't know if I closed the door behind me. Gotta go. See you in the morning. Thanks for the recipe translation," as Brie handed it to her.

After Olive left, Brie and I took dishes of ice cream out onto the balcony and stood looking out into the night sky over the ocean and beach. The beach bar was hopping. A few airplanes came in for a landing. A yacht or two went by. Birds called good night.

I put my arm around Brie. "This is why we come here. This is why we worked so hard all those years, so we could come here. This is our life. I never imagined it would be like this. I feel so very grateful."

"Mmmm, yes," Brie agreed.

"And let's not forget smart. We were smart, too. You taught me how to actually save and invest money. That was a totally foreign concept to me when we met. You were definitely a great find. Thank you for that."

"Mmmm." Brie mulled over what I had said. "Smart and lucky." She hugged me around the waist, then went inside carrying the empty ice cream dishes and spoons.

Chapter Thirteen

The next day, Coco stayed on Saint Martin to observe doctors and local herbalists work as a team. She was particularly interested in the dignity and respect among them for the betterment of their shared patients. The conference participants had options. They could go to the hospital or they could go to the orphanage to take DNA samples from each child. Then participants would work with a permanent crew to compare those results with big DNA sites such as Ancestry. The nearby islands also had their police information that might be helpful in re-creating records for the children.

Brie, Olive, and I went over to Saba for a touring day. The boat ride over was fast and choppy but adventurous. Poor Olive turned green and headed for the center of the boat to lie down. She moaned and managed to keep her dignity. I kept my eyes on the approaching island, something stable so I didn't get dizzy. Brie had her binoculars and bird book. She had a swell time of it. She chatted up other birders. She was in her glory.

Landing on the public dock, I was struck by how steep this island was. We loaded into a van. Our guide told us how Mr. Joseph Lambert Hassel had wanted to build a road on Saba but every engineer and road builder said it couldn't be done. Anyone who knew anything about building a road would not touch the project. So Mr. Hassel and his crew started blowing a road around and up the island. As my father would say, "You don't want to be drunk and have to drive that road at night." It was curvy, to say the least. Our driver was fearless. We rode up to the top of Mount Scenery into a small parking lot.

Here we could either simply ride back down and walk around the small town or walk the eight hundred moss- and lichen-covered steps from The Ladder to The Bottom. Before the road was built, all materials delivered by boat had to be carried up those steps. It was eighty-five degrees and these stairs were through the forest. Think tropical rain forest, damp and muggy and hot.

I immediately said no thanks. Brie, with her post-athletic knees and hips, agreed with my decision. Olive? She was up for this adventure! Several others took the stairs. They had a sixteen-ounce bottle of water each. There was a family of Mom, Dad, a boy of about twelve, and a girl of about nine. There were two other single women with Olive. None of them were fit for this. None of these gals were wearing yoga pants and sports bras. Off they went.

After the hair-raising ride back down, Brie and I walked around in the tiny village. We had a cone of coconut and guava berry ice cream. In a funky little clothing and everything-nice store, we chatted with the owner. Scarves and skirts with hand-sewn embellishments, books about the island's history, hats for men and women, and gift packs of their brand of island rum. (Their recipe is big on cinnamon.) We bought a Christmas tree ornament as our souvenir. I had sweat dripping down my forehead and sides by this time.

I saw the motion sickness remedies and bought some for both Olive and me. So thoughtful.

Then we meandered over to the restaurant where we would all meet up. Blissfully, it had air conditioning. We were first to arrive. We took the recommendation to have a shot of their island rum. Brie and I are not straight liquor drinkers. We like our mixes. I watched enough shots being swallowed with a beer chaser as a child to have a wary feeling about this, but, hey, we were on Saba Island. When would that ever happen again? So we ordered one shot and we split it. Picture a single shot glass and the two of us sipping in turn. The owner tapped the shoulder of the waitress, who tapped the shoulder of the bartender. They couldn't believe what they were seeing. Brie and I gasped, oohed, and delighted in the flavors and warmth.

Let me tell you, it was magically delicious. The cinnamon and sugar gave it a smoothness with some heat. It hit my belly like a small bomb—maybe firecracker is a better way to describe it. Not awful. No pain or gastric disturbances. Like a pebble hitting a puddle and the ripples radiating outward. Yes, that's it. The almost hot ripple that first cleared my sinuses and then traveled throughout my body.

We each ordered a shot for ourselves. Just then, the stair-walking crew dragged themselves through the doors.

They looked awful.

Their clothes stuck to them all over. They were pale and moving slowly. One of the kids was sniffling. Olive had her hiking sandals on. They had a good tread and Olive's feet were stable within all those straps, but the constant downward stepping had created several dark, red spots. Another woman had on white Keds and those little white ankle socks. Those had barely any tread, and she had slipped and slid precariously down several stairs before she simply sat down and cried. She took off her sneakers and went the rest of the way down in her stocking feet. Those socks were black and green from the moss and lichen, and they were soaked through. They were headed for the trash. This woman was more than worn out. She was already starting to ache. Too much.

"That was the most beautiful and stupid thing I've ever done. I was afraid, actually afraid, that I might die on those stairs. It would either be from falling down them because I had on absolutely the wrong footwear or my heart would give out because it was so strenuous. There wasn't a breath of air after the first fifty steps. But once we committed, there was no turning back. We knew the van had already gone back down."

I unstrapped Olive's sandals and let them drop to the floor. I got cool, wet napkins and put them on her neck and wrists. She started to cool down, but she was beat. "My legs feel like jelly. I thought I was going to have a heart attack. What was I thinking?"

The restaurateur gave everyone a large glass of ice water and for those who wanted, a shot of his island rum. Brie and I highly recommended it. Olive went with a decaf iced tea. The father of the family drank his and his wife's shots. Lunch was the Saba Island version of Filet-O-Fish—coconut-encrusted whitefish with lettuce, tomato, and a house-made tartar sauce. The bread was a French brioche. I passed on the French fries to save room for the dessert of coconut ice cream with praline sauce and a drizzle of chocolate. Heaven.

Back in the van, we rode down to the public beach. What a carnival of colors and activities. Some of our group went in the water. We sat in lounge chairs under umbrellas and took it all in. The scuba divers were serious here. You have to know what you're doing, and there's no fooling around. The water brought everyone's spirits back up.

Too soon, we loaded back onto the boat for the return trip. Brie handed out the medications and remedies before we boarded the boat. Olive and I took a single Dramamine and put on one of those bracelets with the bead on them that is supposed to keep motion sickness at bay. We sat at the back of the boat and basically took a nap the whole ride back.

We had just enough time to shower before heading out to meet Coco at the hospital. We were going to try a different part of the island for dinner.

Coco met us in the lobby of the slightly air-conditioned hospital. It was mild respite from the heat outside.

"Hi," said Coco. "We did rounds with one of the doctors and saw patients who were being treated with local remedies as well as pharmaceuticals. Their use of integrative therapy is effective at so many levels. My head and heart are about to burst with it all."

"What was the best part?" I asked.

"The patients looked comfortable and assured with both providers in the room. Yes, that was the best part," Coco said.

As we turned to leave, Mr. Tipo from the orphanage walked by on his way out. "Good afternoon, American friends. I hope seeing you in this medical facility is not because one of you has been injured or become ill?"

I was flattered that he remembered us from the other day.

"No," I answered, "Our friend Coco is part of a conference, and we're meeting here before dinner. Is one of the children from the orphanage ill? I hope everyone is all right."

"Thank you for asking," he answered. "All of our children are fine, but one of our staff took a fall. You remember her. It was Esther."

Everyone looked stunned. "What?" I said. "Is she all right? What happened? Is there anything we can do?"

"Again, thank you for asking, but I believe we have everything under control at the moment. Esther fell down the stairs on her way to a tunnel. One of the older boys found her. She was barely conscious. It was fortunate she was found when she was. Esther has rather large lump on her head. Her ribs are taped, and one knee will be in a cast when that swelling goes down."

Everyone paused to let the damage sink in.

Mr. Tipo continued, "Those stairs are steep and narrow. Add in Esther's advancing age and we really cannot be surprised."

"Well, I am surprised," said Brie and Olive at the same time.

Brie said, "I was impressed at how easily Esther took those stairs the other day."

Olive added, "Yes, I could tell she had climbed them for years. It was as if she knew each tread's slants and dips like I know the steps into my home. I depended on the lights, but Esther didn't need them. She went along assuredly."

"Yes," Brie said, "I remember thinking she moved like a little mountain goat. Was she carrying anything that may have taken her off balance?"

"No. Perhaps she became light-headed or winded."

"Well," I said, "since we're here, would it be all right with you if we stop in to say hello and wish Esther a speedy recovery?"

Mr. Tipo looked at the four of us for a moment and said, "You could distract Esther from her discomfort while the pain medication has time to help her. I'm sure she would appreciate a few minutes of your time. Have a nice evening, ladies." Mr. Tipo left the hospital lobby, and we went to find out which room Esther was in.

The four of us walked into Esther's hospital room. There were three additional people in the other beds. Esther was laid out in the center of her bed. Shrouded in her snow-white sheets and her pale blue hospital gown, she looked small and frail, not like she had the other day.

The room was off-white with tan curtains, a grayish blue linoleum floor, four hospital beds with four nightstands, and not much else. A single wooden chair for a single, quiet visitor was placed by each bed. We tried to be quiet. We tried to act calm and respectful. We're from working-class New England, so we didn't quite hit the mark. We had on touristy, American vacation clothing so we looked fine but a tad loud, let's say, for the setting.

I took in the view and décor, smiled at the closest patient to Esther, and gestured my plan to borrow the chair. My attempt at French: "*Bonjour, madame, s'il vous plait.*" Not knowing the word for chair, I gestured to it and pointed toward Esther. "*Mi amiga.* No, that's not right. *Moi bon.* What is the word for friend?"

The patient started to laugh but then grabbed at her chest as she set off choking from the laughter. She waved me away, still chuckling.

Brie stood by the window looking out, taking it all in carefully listing all of the vocabulary she would teach me later.

Coco looked at the medical chart hanging on the foot of Esther's bed. She walked with knowing confidence as though she actually worked there, smiling and nodding to the patient kitty-corner from Esther. "*Namaste, madam. Para una momento, por favor,*" she said, taking that chair.

That woman's face was pinched, and she barely moved her head to watch Coco take the chair. She said something to Coco that Coco didn't understand, but Brie heard it and chuckled. Brie made eye contact with the woman and walked toward that bed. They started a little chat in French. I picked out *medicale, touristes,* and a few other words that led me to believe Brie was making a case for not calling a nurse to throw us out of the room. She was left standing during her chat with the woman because Coco had taken that chair.

Olive approached Esther's bed and sat on the nearest chair. Bruised skin is bruised skin whether that skin is the color of cinnamon, egg whites, or olive oil. Broken blood vessels looked as though they should hurt, a lot. Esther had a bruise on her right cheek that was turning into a black eye. Pillows beneath her right hip and shoulder allowed her to keep weight off her tender face but it also kept weight off the bump on the back of her head. A pillow between her knees elevated what must have been the damaged knee. We could see how swollen it was beneath the sheet. There was an odor that didn't smell medicinal but it wasn't bad, either. She winced when she turned, and she held her rib section.

"Hello, Esther. We heard you were here and wanted to say hello. Do you remember us from the tour you gave us a couple days ago?" Olive gathered Esther's hands up in her own.

"Hello, girls. Of course I remember you."

I thought that Esther didn't look as though she remembered us. Her eyes didn't settle on Olive's face as squarely as they had the other day.

She looked at Olive and said, "I'm sorry, but I haven't told Mr. Tipo about your program to educate our children about keeping safe from predators. As you can see, something came up."

Well, I thought, so much for my observational and analytical skills. She remembers more from the other day than I do.

"You'll have to forgive me, girls, I look a fright. This tumble has me rattled. I have an egg where it shouldn't be, one kneecap cracked like a macadamia nut shell, and ribs that are barely doing their job, for heaven's sake. But I expect to be home in a few days." Esther looked around Olive, Coco, and me toward the door. Was she expecting someone?

"Esther," Olive asked, still rubbing Esther's hand, "what happened? How did you fall?"

"Frankly, I don't know. I was going down the stairs into the tunnel toward the dining hall and the next thing I knew, people were picking me up. Ooh! That hurt so much, I thought I was going to snap in two. At one point, I was wishing I would so the pain would end."

She closed her eyes and took a breath before she continued. "The medics did their best and were as gentle as could be to lift me onto the stretcher. Narrow stairs and healthy, burly medics along with the child who found me made for cramped movement." She winced at the memory of it.

"That poor child who found me must have gotten the scare of his life. Little David. He was scared and sad. I will thank him and let him know how well I am healing because of his bravery and quick thinking," she said as if making a list of things to do.

She went on, "Then everything went black. I woke up here and I have all these breaks, bruises, bandages, and such a headache. You young people would probably compare this headache with a very bad hangover. I didn't even have a night of fun and frolic." She tried to chuckle as she took a breath.

"So you were going down the stairs," I prompted.

"Yes."

"And you were using the handrail?"

"Yes, I always do. Although I don't need it! But I keep Mr. Tipo from worry by using those handrails."

"Were the stairs wet or were some of the lightbulbs out?"

"No. Jose, our custodian, is diligent about those stairs. They're old but always dry, and a lightbulb is never out for long."

"Oh," she touched the back of her head, grazing a bandage. "I'll bet it will take a while for my hair to grow back in. Eww, it smarts."

"I bet it does hurt, Esther," I sympathized. "Have the doctors given you something for your pain? That bump with your hair shaved around it looks like a little mountain. Is that a salve I see on it?"

Coco explained, "It's a poultice to keep germs out, let the skin rest, and help bring the swelling down. There's an ice pack on the bedside table, too." Olive picked it up and placed it gently on the bump. Esther gave a little sigh of relief after she winced.

Olive remarked, "Esther, I was shocked to hear that you had fallen on those stairs. You were so agile when you gave us the tour. It is odd to even consider that you fell forward but you didn't trip or faint."

"It is odd, my dear. I have been walking those stairs for decades and never slipped on one of them. Maybe I have to admit that I'm getting old."

"What's odd, Esther," I said, "is that you were going down the stairs but you hit the back of your head. It doesn't make sense that you didn't hit the front of your head, don't you think?"

"Maybe it doesn't, I don't know." She glanced again at the door. She looked really tired. We had overstayed our visit.

Olive changed the subject. "Let's talk about getting better and having nice times once you've recovered. What do you enjoy doing when you're not working, Esther?"

"I don't know." She gave it some thought. "I like riding my bicycle. I like reading, and I never miss an opportunity to see our children dance and sing. Occasionally, I sit in the rear of the rehearsal hall and just watch and listen. Sometimes, I sing along without realizing it until Donna gives me a look or the children giggle. Donna takes rehearsal seriously, and at times like that she'll give me a look that could kill. But I'm used to that look. Donna is Donna as only she can be." Esther yawned.

"Donna barked at Esperanza the other day," I said, "but as soon as she caught your eye, she changed her attitude."

Olive caught my eye with her look of "Shut up and let the woman sleep!" I remained seated and listening.

Esther gave a little smile. "I am the only person left who has known Donna all of her life. There isn't anything I don't know about her. Like an old aunt—sometimes she loves me and sometimes she could easily be rid of me. Donna wants to be known for who she has become; what she has made of herself. But I know that none of us can escape or erase our past. Every detail, good or bad, makes us who we are today."

We all nodded in agreement.

"Many of our children are ashamed of their backgrounds, although they had nothing to do with it. Some of them are resilient enough to claim their history, as much as they know of it, and move upward and onto a nice life filled with love and safety. Some cannot." She yawned and her eyes closed briefly before she continued.

"I remember when Donna was born. I brought her to St. Emiliani's. The mother succumbed just after the birth." Esther's eyes closed again for a couple of seconds and then she went on. "She was a Haitian beauty and just whimpered." Esther gave a big yawn. "The mother wasn't making any sense. But I dutifully wrote her dying words on the back of the Certificate of Live Birth. Now those records are gone. I am old. Once I am gone, no one will know Donna's birth story. It is better Donna not learn that her mother lost her mind during birth."

Olive said, "Maybe it was a true story, Esther. Donna wouldn't be the first child born from an affair."

Esther gave a wave as though to dismiss Olive's thought. Olive sat back in her chair with a bit of a scowl on her face. Doesn't she loathe injustice.

"Esther, how did Donna get her name? Donna doesn't sound like a Caribbean kind of name. Did her mother name her in her dying breath?" I asked. Olive rolled her eyes at my drama.

"I named her," Esther yawned again.

Olive said, "We have exhausted you, Esther, and you're supposed to be resting. I'm sorry to have kept you awake, but your stories are fascinating. We'll go now. Take care of yourself."

"Good bye, girls," Esther said as her eyes closed yet again.

We put our chairs back where they belonged with as little noise as we could. As we turned to leave the room, standing in the doorway was Detective Pamela.

"Get into my cruiser now," she ordered through gritted teeth. Then she looked down at the opened notepad. The page was covered in writing, and her left hand fidgeted with her pen.

Coco asked, "Get any good intel there, Detective?"

The detective escorted us down the hallway and out the lobby doors. "No talking until we get to the police station. I have had about all I can take from you four."

Brie sent me a look that could kill. Gosh, she hates getting into trouble. We passed a TV news van on our way out of the parking lot.

"Now, Detective—" I began.

Brie and Olive each clamped a hand over my mouth before I could utter another sound.

Once we were seated in a conference room at the police station, Detective Pamela came in, accompanied by another female officer. Both had their notepads open and pens ready.

I bit my lip to keep quiet and allow the detective to run the interview. But I was dying of curiosity. I sat up straight in my chair and placed my clasped hands on the table.

There was barely a breath of air in the room.

Detective Pamela began. "I have had a moment to collect my thoughts. You are here at my request."

My anxiety turned defensive and anger burped out of me. "It didn't sound as though we had a choice back at the hospital, Detective."

"Tssst!" Olive warned me to be quiet.

"As I was saying," Detective Pamela continued as if I hadn't spoken, "you are here by invitation. This officer will take you back to your vehicle at any time, but I hope you will remain here and tell me what you were doing interrogating Miss Esther. Since I have made it clear," she laid her palm flat on the table, "that you should use your time on Saint Martin to rest, eat, and have fun. I find it troubling that again," she nodded her head for emphasis, "during my investigation, to find the four of you in the middle of it."

I bit my lip, hoping someone else would say something. I counted quickly to three and couldn't wait any longer. "Detective, we spoke with you on Sunday and had no plans to see you again, but on Monday, three of us went to the Butterfly Farm, then Loterie Farm in Pic Paradis for lunch."

My rate of speech was increasing. Even I could hear it, but I kept going.

"On the way home, we saw the orphanage and stopped to take a look. Mr. Tipo had Esther give us a tour. He was so gracious, and she was so sweet." I extended my hand across the table toward the detective. She made no move to close the distance between us.

I brought my hand back to my edge of the table and continued. "Today, we met Coco at the hospital to have dinner in a different part of the island, just as we told you we would be doing from now on. I mean, really, Detective—"

The detective's eyebrow shot up and froze me solid. Her warning look stopped me in my glib tracks. I nodded in apology for my informality and continued.

"We are not trying to be part of this investigation, but information just drops in our laps." I sat back and brought my hands up in helplessness. "So anyway," I continued, "we were at the hospital, ready to go out to dinner, and Mr. Tipo told us about Esther, so we stopped in to wish her well. And we got to talking and she got to telling us stories."

Detective Pamela started to speak, and I zipped it. "Let me remind you once again; you do not have to try to remove yourselves from this investigation because you are not part of it. For some reason, or perhaps many, you repeatedly appear at places, talking with people from the island who are of interest in this, MY investigation." She took a deep breath and looked over to her colleague. The colleague was biting her top lip and nodded to Detective Pamela.

The detective continued. "You said 'stories'? Did she tell you information beyond what she shared today? What did she tell you while you toured the orphanage?"

Olive put her hand on my arm and leaned forward, toward the detective. "She told us how great Donna is with the kids and to the orphanage as a whole. They adore her. She has the run of the place most of the time, either working with the kids or developing her own act. We interrupted her rehearsal with the kids, and Donna barked at us. She started to get into it with one of the girls, but she caught

Esther's leveling gaze and checked herself. It was as though she turned on a dime—she went from angry to kind and benevolent, just like that." She snapped her fingers.

Brie said, "I watched Esther go up and down those stairs without any trouble or hesitation. I was jealous. I have been athletic all of my life, and barrel jumping and soccer have taken their toll on my knees. Those stairs were getting brutal by the end of the tour, but Esther showed no sign of fatigue or of having trouble at all on those stairs. I find it difficult to believe, Detective, that she fell down those stairs."

"And," I added, "if Esther fell down the steps, how did she get the bump on the back of her head? If she fell, she fell forward, right? Why isn't the bump on her forehead? I'm not buyin' it," I said.

Detective Pamela took a deep breath and, glanced at her colleague then back to me. "It is not up to you to be *buyin'* anything." She was mimicking me. "Remember, this is a criminal investigation. If necessary, I will ask you questions that you will answer simply and without your impressions."

I looked down at my right hand. It didn't sting, but I could have sworn it had just been slapped. I felt truly chagrinned. My father would have gritted his teeth and said, "Ya just can't keep your mouth shut, can ya?"

Detective Pamela saw my shamed face and took yet another deep breath. "I received a call from the hospital doctor after he examined Esther. There were some inconsistencies between the report and her injuries. They took X-rays and photographs of the area on her head as well as her other injuries from the fall. That is why I was at the hospital."

"What have they found?" Coco blurted. Olive swatted her arm.

"It is none of your concern. Thank you for sharing what you have learned. I also am grateful that Esther felt comfortable telling you about Donna's birth. That is interesting."

I knew enough not to ask any more questions, but my eyebrows went up as my head cocked to one side. I simply waited.

"Again, that is not for your entertainment. It is part of the investigation," Detective Pamela concluded. "Now I will ask Officer DuBois to return you to your vehicle at the hospital."

We started to stand up, scraping metal chairs on concrete while being careful of our balance and any sore muscles.

"Let me be clear," Detective Pamela said, stopping us mid-move, "that I do not want you to interfere with Miss Esther's recuperation again. I believe your tour questions have been sufficiently answered so you have no reason to see her again. Am I making myself clear?"

We each nodded to her.

Officer DuBois said, "I'll keep a list of names of anyone attempting to enter Miss Esther's room."

Detective Pamela's eyes flew up from her notebook on the table to the officer's.

Officer DuBois' face fell and her eyes closed momentarily as she realized she had just let information slip.

"So," surmised Coco, "you're putting an officer by Miss Esther's room, eh? Such care you're providing the dear old bird for just a slip down a stairwell."

"Good night, ladies. Enjoy your dinner," Detective Pamela Poissonier said, ignoring Coco's comment. She stood and turned toward the door.

"Hey, Detective," I asked, trying to convey a friendly, touristy curiosity, "where do you go for dinner? We're looking for someplace not-so-touristy but that will put up with us since, you know, we are tourists."

"Ladies, as a detective, I keep my personal time private. I go out to dinner at places very few others go to for specifically that reason. Tonight, I plan to update my report and go home."

"Oh, what do you do to unwind and relax?" Olive asked. "With your job, you must have high stress. How do you manage that? Meditation? Yoga? Alcohol? Kickboxing? Do you use any herbal therapies like Rescue Remedy? I bet that would help you. I use it sometimes."

Officer DuBois wrote as she repeated, "Rescue Remedy. Got it. I'll be sure to remind you of that later, Detective." She smiled at the detective as she ushered us out of the conference room behind Detective Pamela.

As we walked down the precinct hallway, I watched the detective go into her office, close the door, and then shut the blinds of her windows. Walking by her door, I thought I heard a groan coming from her office.

Chapter Fourteen

Officer Sharon DuBois led us out of the police station and into her cruiser. She rolled that cruiser out of the lot and into traffic as if she were driving a limousine. Such a smooth ride. We all chuckled when cars in front of us would notice the cruiser in their rearview mirror and suddenly slow down. On the quieter streets, with her window open, Officer DuBois would smile and wave at residents. Some of them knew her by name.

"Hey, Officer D, you giving tours of the neighborhood now?" one said.

Another chimed in, "Money must be tight at the station, eh?"

"Oh yes," she said with a smile, "I am showing off the fine young people of our town."

"You have found them!" Clutching the handlebars of his bike, the boy popped a wheelie and spun his front tire around. "Officer D and tourist friends, take my picture. It will help raise my aspirations for a brighter tomorrow!" His buddy was laughing too hard to say or do anything. The traffic light changed, and we drove away from the boys.

"It looks as though you are the favorite neighborhood cop," Coco commented from the front passenger seat.

"I am, until someone strays out of line. Then I quickly become the least favorite. On my beat, the families know I come around on Friday nights to check in and give positive reports on family members."

"Really? You do that every week?" I asked.

"Yes, I go to a different area each Friday of the month so I cover the whole beat in a month's time. I mix up the order each month so families don't know which Friday I may visit them. I picked Friday nights because that has been the night when people cause the most mischief, shall we say. For some families, the idea of a happy officer paying them a visit is enough to keep people home and behaving well. Some parents keep a closer watch over their adolescent children. We've seen the number of incidences go down since we started this pilot program."

"Wow," said Brie, "that sounds like an amazing program. Are you the only department doing this?"

"Yes, I am the only officer doing this. Pam, er, Detective Poissonier and I spent time looking at our data and developed this concept along the theory of intermittent positive reinforcement, and our initial data is proving our point."

"How are you liking this new part of your job? How does it feel to collect, record, and report back to families about the good things their children and the parents themselves are doing?" I asked. "And how is it different when you have to report bad behavior? I expect that has changed with families you've gotten to know better through this program, right?"

"Your observation is accurate. Detective Poissonier and I identified the families with the highest number of incidences including out-of-the-home illegal activity and in-home domestic abuse or neglect. When we identified those families, we looked at the juvenile records from the schools that have involved the police. We added an At Risk factor into the data. When families see me approaching their home on a Friday, they beam with pride. When I knock on their door during the week, they are not so happy to see me. Depending on why I am there during the week and who answers the door, it can go well or it may escalate quickly."

"Like a child who tears up the note from the teacher to the parent for bad behavior, that same juvenile might try to beat his parents to the door and get rid of you before his parents see you, right?" Olive asked. "Do you work with the school guidance counselors? Oh, do the schools have guidance counselors?"

"Our school principals met with us when we developed this program. They could not share confidential information, of course. We showed them street maps, and they identified which neighborhoods suffered the most trouble with abuse, hunger, neglect, and drugs. When their identification of neighborhoods matched our data, we knew we were on the right track. Our proposal includes permission to share information across schools and hospitals."

"This sounds like more than a couple of glasses of wine after a shift, Officer DuBois," Coco said. "You and Pam, is it? You and Pam must spend a lot of time together. What is she like after hours? Come on, you can tell us."

"Oh no, I cannot tell you. Detective Poissonier is a highly diligent and professional law enforcement officer. She would waste no time in pinning me to the mat next time we train together if I speak about her personally."

She added, "I can tell you that she is a good woman. She was the first to bring this data to my attention and invite me to analyze it with her. She had identified places where her work overlapped in my beat. She had already created the spreadsheet of addresses, names of family members, with their dates of birth, where they may be employed, prior arrests, and other data. When we looked at just that, we could see patterns in some families. I recognized some of the names and addresses. When she explained her idea to use praise and positive attention to drive down at-risk and illegal behavior, I jumped on board right away."

"Detective Poissonier. Okay, everyone, from now on we call her by her title and full last name, okay?" Olive said. The rest of us agreed. "Good. Criminy, she's right out straight, isn't she? Does she ever take time off? How does she keep going? This could burn her out in no time."

"Oh, don't worry. Detective Poissonier has effective strategies to maintain her mental and spiritual health. The two of us along with other women on the island who are in law enforcement have our own support group, you might call it, but we are not that organized. A few detectives started getting together at conferences and island-level meetings. They would take time to talk and check in with one another, and then they began inviting officers into the group. We see those in our precincts regularly, and if necessary—say one of us gets injured or ill or pregnant—the email goes out and we all rally for that woman. Your information, Miss Olive, about the herbal supplements will be well received. I will pick some up before work tomorrow and put them on Detective P's desk. That is as much to drive her a little crazy as to help keep her calm."

"Don't get yourself in trouble, Officer DuBois," Olive warned.

"I am not worried. Detective P may pin me the first time, but I would get my licks in before we were through," Officer Dubois chuckled at the thought of it.

"Okay," said Coco, "now, where do you suggest we go for dinner?"

"Oh my, I know of just the place, and it is not too very far from here. My cousin Danny has a place on the beach. There will be live music and cold drinks and the snappiest grilled shrimp you have ever eaten. When we stop, I will text you the address and you may use your GPS to help you find it, but it is easy to find from the hospital. Just go down the main boulevard until you see signs for Cinnamon Bay. Go there. As you drive down the road that borders the beaches, you will pass a beach that is family-friendly. The sign will show the silhouettes of a family. Then you will pass an adult-only beach. That means clothing optional. The sign will show only an adult male and adult female. After that, you will come to my cousin's restaurant on the beach. He calls it Toucan Sam's Beach Bar and Grille. It has a colorful sign. Tell Danny that I sent you and to give you a table out of the way. I recommend the rice, however he is making it tonight."

Officer DuBois parked her cruiser in the hospital parking lot and escorted us to our rental car. "It has been interesting getting to know you, ladies. Have a pleasant and quiet time for the remainder of your time on Saint Martin. I trust Detective Poissonier will not be seeing you again."

"Well," I said, "you never know what might happen in our last couple of days here—where we'll be, what we'll do, or who we'll run into."

"Please," Officer Dubois interrupted, "do your best not to run into Detective Poissonier. Now, as I told her, I will stand here until you are all in your vehicle and have driven off the hospital grounds. I hope you enjoy my cousin's restaurant. Do you remember how to get there?"

"Yes, past the clothing-optional beach and look for Toucan Sam's Beach Bar and Grille right after that. A colorful sign should take out any guesswork. Thank you for all of your help this afternoon."

"It's all part of the service. And," she leaned into the car at Olive, "thank you for the information on Rescue Remedy for the detective. I might try it myself."

I drove out of the hospital parking lot and into the evening traffic, which was heavy. There was tension in the car after the last few hours of discovery with Esther and the good detective. Olive acted on it.

"Why doesn't everyone except Vidalia close her eyes, and let's take a deep breath in, hold it for five-four-three-two-one, and let it out slowly. We're regaining our natural breathing rhythm after these hours in the hospital and then the police station. Okay, as you slowly take in another deep breath, picture the air as clean and colorful. Pick your own color as long as it's clean, calm, and safe. Hold it for five. Now as you slowly let it out, let that breath carry your worries, tension, and fears with it. Remember that what has happened is in the past and nothing can be re-done or done about it so let it go. Remind yourself that you are in Saint Martin, it's eighty-three degrees, and we're headed for delicious food and atmosphere on a beach with no snow. Let's all take those breaths three times and see how we feel afterward."

Coco and Brie fell right in line with Olive's exercise. I took deep breaths and imagined the color apricot going in and the negative going out while I kept my eyes on the road and other drivers.

After the next three breaths, Brie started to chuckle, which is always a good sign that she is relaxing.

"Olive, you are a godsend right now. If it was just your sister and me here and she'd gotten us escorted to the police station, I don't think I could have calmed down enough to go out for dinner. More than likely I would have shut down, been exhausted, gotten all caught up in what might have happened, and just been a bear to be around. But the breathing gave me time to see that all of that is over, that we didn't get into any real trouble, and I'm actually quite hungry. So thank you."

"Aww!" Olive said, putting her hand to her chest.

The car was quiet for a few minutes as I negotiated from the main boulevard to a secondary road and finally down to the beach road. Sure enough, there was Toucan Sam's right where we were told we would find it. I swung into a parking space. Relieved, happy, and hungry, our foursome got out and headed for the wraparound porch with tiki torches lining pathways and twinkle lights under umbrellas and the porch roof.

I was in the lead, as I often am, when we reached the top step to the porch. A light-tan skinned man in his early thirties with crop-cut black hair, a moustache, and sparkling brown eyes came up to the group with a big, welcoming smile.

"You must be the women with the food names, am I right?" he asked as he extended his hand to shake each of ours in turn. "I am Danny DuBois, the owner and operator of this fine establishment. I have just received word on high authority that I am to take excellent care of you. I have also been ordered to keep you here and 'out of trouble.' Perhaps you can tell me what that means over your first beverage. Let me show you to your table."

He turned and led us to a table in a corner of the porch with a view of the ocean. The porch was raised by four steps and built on stilts. There were a few cabanas on the beach with their own tiki torches, ice buckets, and tables for food. Very romantic.

We were gleeful. This was exactly what Brie and I had envisioned for this trip. Olive kept the conversation going with Danny. "So, your higher authority wouldn't be your cousin Officer DuBois, would it?"

"Oh yes," Danny answered. "When she identifies herself on the phone as Officer and not Sharon, I know she is all business and doesn't have a lot of time to chitchat. When the officer calls, I listen and do as told. We often have families from her new project here as a reward. No, Sharon slaps my hand with that word *reward*. We do not reward appropriate behavior, we *ree-in-force* it. Anyway, about once a month I get a call and one of her families arrives for a dinner. They have a coupon from the program, and I give them a great discount. I tell them it is for keeping my cousin safe, happy, and employed. We all get a laugh at her expense. It warms my heart to hear their stories and how my cousin is helping them."

"I'll bet it feels great to have a family member doing such remarkable work. And you must feel pretty good, too, that she has asked you to be a part of it. She must feel you have the right personality and heart for the project," Coco said.

"Oh yeah, I am the salt of the earth," Danny said, taking a sweeping bow.

We all laughed at the twinkle in his eye.

"Oh yes, Danny is the salt of the earth, the salt on the rim of my margarita, and the salt in my coffee this morning, thank you very much, you mischief-maker," a nearby waitress called out.

"One reason why I always have a second shirt in my office. She spat the mouthful of salted coffee all over me. My darling Veronique, you didn't give me time to add the caramel. You see, it is all your own fault for your lack of patience." He winked at us with a wide grin.

"I am the one who lacks patience?" Veronique retorted with one eyebrow raised. Danny's face fell with a look of someone who had just stepped into a mess of his own making.

"I know that look. Your butt is grass, buddy, and she has the lawn mower," Coco summed up the situation.

The waitress cracked a wide grin as she walked by, slapping Danny on his bottom. She stopped long enough to plant a kiss on his cheek. Veronique walked away with a tight hip-sashaying salsa walk. Danny winced.

"What did you do? Or rather, what haven't you done?" I asked.

"Mon Dieu," Danny pleaded as he put his hand over his heart. "That is the woman of my life. Not only is she physically every man's dream, but her heart and spirit are equal in beauty. She was referring to her patience waiting for my marriage proposal. We have been together for a few years. Veronique helped me dream this restaurant into reality. She is the one with the ideas and plans to decorate and light the cabanas on the beach. This place would not be as big or as wonderful as it is without her."

"Well, at least make her a financial partner, if you haven't already," Brie said.

"Wait a minute," I interrupted, "you would be smart to propose marriage and add the financial piece in after she accepts. If you offer her a partnership instead of a marriage, she may be more than insulted and hurt. She wants the commitment of love. Then add the financial piece."

"Oh my goodness, Sharon said you were a force to be reckoned with, but I had no idea my future would be laid out for me by four ladies from America. I will take it all under advisement. But now, let's get something tall, cool, and wet for you as you look over the menu. I will send a waitress, not Veronique, to your table." Danny walked away with a bit of a wobble, holding his head with one hand, steadying himself on tables with the other.

We laughed until we cried.

Four ice waters arrived and we gulped them down. We hadn't realized it had been hours since we'd had anything to drink. Two chilled white wines, an ice-cold Corona, and an iced tea with strawberry garnish came next. This was Caribbean relaxation.

Out on the beach, a few large lights strung up into the trees came on. A man started setting up a speaker, mic stands, and a stool. He worked steadily and with purpose. A few strings of lights, twinkle lights this time, came on. When they did, the man looked up at the porch with a smile.

"No!" I whispered. I looked around for Danny or Veronique. I wanted someone to be our witnesses. Because when Detective Poissonier found out that Dru was about to perform right in front of us, I wanted someone to be able to vouch for us.

"Detective P is not going to be happy with this, nor will she probably believe it," Brie said.

"We may as well drive straight to the airport when we leave here," Coco chuckled.

Olive said, "Just don't look him in the eye. Maybe he won't notice us. It'll be fine."

Dru didn't appear to have seen us. He brought out a second stool. He set up an electric piano, pulled out a few different drums and a guitar. Every few minutes, he would look toward the entrance he had used.

When everything was arranged, Dru looked up to find Danny. Dru tapped his watch and shrugged his shoulders, holding up his hands as if asking for guidance. Then he whisked his hands to one side as if tossing away whatever weight he'd been holding.

Dru walked over to one of the microphones, pulled it out of its holder, and clicked it on.

"Good evening, ladies and gentlemen! How are you doing tonight? Isn't this a beautiful evening for delicious food, friends, and family with the sounds of the ocean in the background?"

People nodded, and a few applauded.

Dru continued. "I am Dru LeBlanc, and I will be performing for you this evening. We may have another guest a little later, but I have been assured once or twice," he moved his left hand down and over his skin-tight slacks down his hip, "that I am more than enough on my own, if you know what I mean." He winked at the people on the porch. Then he flipped a few switches on the piano and background music came up.

"Let's get happy!" he shouted and started singing Luke Bryan's "Play It Again."

People started to bop in their seats and sing along with the chorus. It was the first song of his set, and we were sweating. Dru swung into George Strait's "I Got a Car" when our dinners arrived.

Olive said, "Okay, we're just going to enjoy our vacation and not worry about any police investigation. We're here. Dru is here. So what? The music is so good, and this food looks amazing."

The rice of the night was a mix of white and wild rice seasoned with a jerk-type seasoning of onion, thyme, cinnamon, some hot pepper, paprika, cumin, and garlic. It was robust and flavorful. Black, and garbanzo beans were in it, too. To finish it off, there were bite-sized pieces of mango in it. The sweet with the heat was perfectly balanced for me. The dish wasn't finished there.

The rice mixture was mounded in the center of the dish. Grilled shrimp, pulled pork, bite-sized pieces of beef, and whitefish ringed the rice. I had to hold myself back from throwing my face completely into the plate, it looked and smelled so good. The kind of thing you could keep eating until you exploded, and you'd die wanting more.

Dru was crooning through "Am I Wrong" by Nico & Vinz. Brie clicked her iPad to record the performance. Oh, he made them proud with his rendition on the piano and his aching voice.

"What a great set of lyrics," Coco said. "Any minority can relate to this. Anyone who simply doesn't have enough love, opportunity, breaks, or money. This guy is really good."

Dru took a short break. Before he left the beach area, he pulled out his cell phone and punched in a number. He didn't look happy as he rounded the corner, out of sight. Danny leaned over the porch railing and handed Dru a beer as he flipped the spotlights off.

And we continued eating.

Danny had a pistou, a Jamaican-influenced sauce from France that I used as a dipping sauce for some of the meats. It's kind of like pesto here in the US, but instead of Parmesan cheese, they used shredded Gouda. It was a spiritual experience, let me tell you.

When Coco's whole grilled redfish arrived, complete with its eyes still in its head that were now smoke-filled was laid before her, I actually let out an "Eek!" I am not usually a screamer, but this was like nothing I had ever seen. Everyone chuckled at my reaction. Thankfully, Coco covered the head with her napkin. I couldn't bear watching those eyes as she tore into the body. We all took a bite and it was very good. Small dishes of olives and pickled vegetables made Coco delirious.

As I took a breather from eating, Dru came back onto the beach. Alone. As the spotlights came back on, Dru tossed his shoulders back and sprinted the rest of the way to his microphone like a political candidate. He took the mic from its stand and walked up the steps and onto the porch.

"I am back and am happy to see you all still here!" He looked at each table. He saw and recognized us and beamed. "Hello, my dear friends from Maine, America!" Dru came over to our table and shook hands with each of us. "I looked online to see where Maine is." He paused. "It looks very cold but beautiful."

Then he added in a low voice to bring the audience closer, "You are about to see how I perform under pressure. I will tell you a little story about performing. Sometimes, I perform with one other person or an entire group. We rehearse and perfect each song. Many times, I will sing a duet with a lovely lady and sometimes, I am simply backup. But every song is rehearsed from the first note to the last. Choreography, too." He looked at his feet and shook his head.

"And sometimes, something happens to upend the entire show. For example, let's just say for this story, the other performer does not," he looked both ways, "arrive for the show. And let's just say, for example, that there is no answer on her phone and no one who also knows her has any information that will help me give you the performance as rehearsed." Dru rocked back and forth from his heels to his toes several times.

"You know that saying 'The show must go on'? Well, ha ha, this one is going to. Yes, it is going to."

He jumped off the top step onto the sand. He flipped a couple of switches on the piano, then came around to the front of it and planted his feet.

"Now this next song was to be performed by my partner. You know, the one who is not here." He gestured one hand up and down beside him to indicate the empty space. "So I will do my best and definitely have some fun while bringing you Taylor Swift's song "Shake It Off."

Brie started recording this.

Up came the intro, and he placed himself in ballet positions that weren't half bad. He was great when the hip-hop dancers' part came. And the ribbon dancing was, as it was for Taylor Swift, a hysterical bomb. Dru was all over that beach. He had sand flying with his kicks and leaps. Those of us on the porch were shaking our hands during the chorus. Even Brie, who didn't know the song, was shaking her hands to shake off the haters.

"He will get a lot of tips just for taking that song on. Oh, what a good sport he is," I said.

"He'll probably make it a regular number in his solo act after this!" Olive said. "The lyrics fit any gender, and his antics are so funny."

Brie gave Dru a thumbs-up. "I'll call my colleagues at the opera house for contact information at the Ogunquit Playhouse. They should be able to connect with Dru for guidance. He's got Broadway musical written all over him, doesn't he?"

During all of this, our attentive waitress was friendly and efficient. Water glasses were never lower than a third full. After she asked twice about another round of alcohol and we declined, she stopped asking. She was casual about upselling us on different small plates when she realized that was our weakness. We passed on the squid and oysters but fell prey to the cinnamon sugar pecans and a crème brûlée to share.

Dru finished up with John Legend's "All of Me." A good romantic song to send lovers home for the night. Danny and Veronique were dancing.

"With that song, I doubt Dru will be going home alone tonight," I said, smiling. "Neither will Veronique and Danny. Those two seem to have all the pieces of a solid relationship. They've already taken risks with each other. They have trust, experience, and love. Maybe I'll suggest that Dru sing Billy Joel's 'Tell Her About It.'"

Before I could move to get up from my chair, three hands held me down.

"No!"

"You are not going to speak to Dru!"

"You're not going anywhere near him!"

They each felt rather strongly about my staying away from Dru.

"Okay, I won't talk with him. It's not as though I would bring up the death of his girlfriend. But since you three brought it up, who do you think he was waiting for tonight?" I sucked in air. "Ooh! Do you think he was waiting for Donna? Do you think something has happened to her? What if she's been killed?"

Brie grabbed my right hand. Olive took my left. Coco stood behind me as I rose from my chair.

"Stop talking, Vidalia. We're getting you out of here before you get us in trouble. Jeesh, do you ever quit?"

Brie grabbed the check from our table. It had a substantial discount "for friends and family." Brie and Coco took care of it while Olive kept me moving toward the exit, telling me to shush. I was giggling by this point.

Olive and I spoke with Veronique on the way out. Danny was watching us.

"Just pretend that we're giving you sound advice. Look serious and interested," I said.

And Veronique did. It was hard not to snicker.

Olive said, "Now look at Danny, smile and wink at him, and then look back at us."

Veronique did just that. Danny started to look worried.

"That's exactly where you want him, Veronique. Keep him guessing a little while telling him exactly what you want. He's getting ready to take the plunge. You just need to provide the dream like you did for this restaurant. He needs your dreams so he can see it work. Good luck and take care," I said.

We walked out to the car and enjoyed a blissful ride back to the resort. I looked in my rearview mirror more than once, making sure I didn't see a police cruiser coming after us.

Chapter Fifteen

It was Wednesday. Drat, we were more than halfway through our vacation. Part of me wanted to do everything possible, and another part wanted to just sit and savor the beauty and heat. With Coco on Saba, Olive, Brie, and I joined a group for a tour of the island that included lunch on a beach. I got to live my kind of luxury. Others took care of every detail.

We loaded onto a van at eight thirty in the morning and had our first delight—the van was air-conditioned. Our tour guide, Priscilla, had lived on Saint Martin all her life. As our agile driver, Bart, maneuvered around construction sites, roadwork, busses, cars, vans, goats, and chickens, Priscilla identified points of interest along the way. She added her life story when possible.

"Here is the little corner store where my friends and I would walk for ice cream after our chores and homework were completed. We would watch the tour busses go by and make up stories about the people riding in them." She looked at us with a grin before going on.

"And here is the church most of my family attended." Priscilla smiled with extra warmth as she retold a story of wearing a wide-brimmed hat held on with an elastic under her chin.

"Mama said it was made especially for little girls who liked to run and jump and constantly lost their sunglasses. With the hat on, Mama said, there was no need for sunglasses, and the chin strap kept it on my head no matter what I thought up to do."

She chuckled. "Oh, Mama hated the years of wearing mantillas to church. For girls like me, mantillas became scarves, which became capes, which became caught up in the wind and gone, all before we got into the church. So Mama always had a napkin or tissue and a bobby pin for such emergencies. How embarrassing!"

"Our first stop is an overlook of Simpson Bay on the way to Phillipsburg." She pointed out Cupecoy further north and nearby Saba Island. She mentioned the large desalination plant down to the right of where we were standing, and I wondered how Bertrand was doing.

Back in the van, we rode down to and through Phillipsburg so we could see the open market and the beach scene. Three cruise ships were anchored offshore so their passengers could spend time shopping and eating. Brie wondered aloud how many of them would tour the government building. Yes, some people actually do that. I smiled at her. She was such an odd duck.

A few miles later, the van pulled into the long, uphill paved driveway to a resort on the east side of the island. We got out of the van to enjoy the view.

Looking out over more of the Caribbean Ocean, we could see Saint Lucia. Elegant sailboats glided below us. The one or two clouds overhead looked so close I reached up to try and touch them. It was perfect weather: eighty-three degrees with a mild breeze off the ocean. I was up on a bluff overlooking more of paradise with two of my favorite people. I took a few minutes to savor, reflect, and feel grateful. Several people were taking selfies. This was a future Christmas card in the making.

Our lunch stop found us at Orient Bay. What a luscious place. If you watch the BBC television show *Death in Paradise,* this could be the setting. We piled out with our bulging beach bags and walked into the thatch-roofed restaurant bar.

The manager welcomed us, and staff served us complimentary beverages of our choice: Corona beer, margaritas, rum punch, or soft drinks. We joined a couple of ladies from the tour at a large picnic table for eight and chatted between sips. We watched children and adults playing in the water, lying in the sun or the shade of their beach umbrella, or making sandcastles. This was heaven on earth, right here, right now. This was what we had come here for.

One by one, we slipped into the changing stalls and into our swimsuits. Even Brie. She applied suntan oil to her French-Canadian olive skin while Olive and I slathered SPF 50 onto our Irish and Scottish freckled pinky-whiteness.

There was a large floating platform out in the water with kids jumping off it. A few young women were attempting to sunbathe, but the drippy and splashing kids were interrupting their bliss. On one end, there was a slide that launched teens about four feet out from the end of the slide into the water. Younger kids didn't go as far. There were squeals of fright and delight.

I had my eye on that slide. After lunch and the required half-hour rest before going into the water, my goal was to actually swim to that raft, climb up the ladder onto that platform, climb another ladder to the top of that slide, and scream my head off on the way down. Yup, that was my plan. Adventure is my middle name.

With my eyes back on the beach, I noticed elementary-aged kids moving toward a pop-up canopy set up at one end of the beach. A tall fellow dressed in khaki shorts, à la Mutual of Omaha's *Wild Kingdom* but with water shoes on, had set up a long table and some kind of equipment. There was some familiarity between the man and some of the kids. The adults with them seemed to know the man, too.

That's when a second man put up an easel signboard with "Saint Martin Department of Water," the island seal, and "Outreach Services" at the bottom. The two men talked with the kids and adults until they were ready to start. Their small public address system was turned on. The taller man picked up a ukulele and sang "I Love Mud" by Rick Charette. Kids and adults in the know sang along.

Olive, Brie, and I walked over to watch. The fellow introduced himself. It was Bertrand D'Lamore!

Bertrand and his assistant, Julio, interacted with adventurous youngsters dripping mud through their fingers and toes as they sang. They finished the song laughing. Bertrand and Julio took clear plastic cups, dipped them in the shallow ocean water, and showed everyone cups full of salty water with some mud and unidentifiable floaty things in it. They held out their glasses, offering them to the audience to drink.

"Would you like a nice cold drink?"

No one took their offer. There were gasps and repulsed facial expressions, stomachs touched as if for protection.

"What is wrong? This is water, isn't it?"

"It's salty and has stuff floating in it," one boy said.

"Yes, but it's gross. People pee in that water," a girl added.

"Ah well, what can we do? Here we are on beautiful Saint Martin surrounded by water but we cannot drink it."

A father added, "You're the water district fellows. Can't you fix it?"

"Well, yes, we can. It is a big secret process. Julio and I are the only two in the whole water district to know how to do this. Can you keep a secret?"

"Oh yes!"

"Okay then. Let's take these two glasses of ocean water that no one wants to drink and see what Julio and I can do. First, let's get the sand, mud, and bigger pieces filtered out." The men poured their water through a coffee-can-size clear plastic container with a tube coming out of the bottom. The clear tube had materials that looked like charcoal and fibers of some kind. The water filtered through it and into a second clear container. We could see the water was now clear.

"It looks better, doesn't it?"

"Yes," many said.

"Now do you want to drink it?"

One or two youngsters started reaching out for the glasses only to be slapped back by the adults who said, "Not yet. Just because it is clear doesn't mean it is clean enough to drink."

"Absolutely correct. Julio and I brought some bottled water from the grocery store. Let's open it and see what is inside."

Bertrand dipped a few different strips of paper into the opened bottle. Julio pointed to a large poster of safe levels of different minerals found in drinking water. The level for salt was highlighted.

"You see that Julio brought the test guide for us. Clean water that is safe to drink has these levels of minerals in it. The bottled water falls into the safe areas. Now let's test our clear ocean water."

Each dipped strip was charted on the poster, showing very unsafe levels of salt and other minerals. Audience members made faces and groaned.

"Well, Julio, now what do we do?" Bertrand turned back to his audience. "Ladies and gentlemen, what do we need to do?"

"You need to get the yuck out!" one youngster cried out.

"Well, Julio, you heard the man. Let's get the yuck out. Let's get a few more filters."

They did, testing as they went and posting the improving results. Audience members were getting excited. The salt level was in the safe zone.

"Now we have some bacteria to get rid of. Julio and I can only do that precise work back at the plant. You have seen how we take the salt out of this beautiful ocean that gives us so much, and with a few more processes back at the plant, this water will be safe to drink."

"I want to drink it now," one young boy squealed.

"Oh, you think you do?" Bertrand winked at an adult man who may have been the boy's father. "Now, Julio, let's test this water a few more times."

Julio dipped test strips into the processed water and used a wide sweep of his arm to show everyone the test-strip results. He charted the results on the poster board. They were still in the danger zone.

"These are the minerals and even some living organisms that are still in this water. I can tell you, you do not want them in your belly. They can make you sick."

"Sometimes," said one young girl, "if I swim all day, I swallow some of the ocean water and then I don't feel very good that night. Is that why?"

"Maybe. Drinking salt water is never a healthy idea. What we wanted to do today was to show you how we get the salt out of the water so you have an appreciation of the science and common sense that is required. Have we done what we planned to do?"

"YES!"

"Good. Thank you very much for your attention and participation this morning. Julio and I have had a good time sharing how this island makes our ocean water clean and safe. Now you know how it is done. And now Julio and I are going to enjoy our lunch here. Thank you and have a wonderful time."

Julio and Bertrand took their time breaking everything down, packing it up, and getting it locked into the water district van. They chatted with kids and adults alike. They "asked" for help from some of the timid but interested youngsters. A few were drawn to the ukulele. Bertrand took time to show one boy how to place his fingers correctly on a fret to make a perfect C chord. A couple of string-bikini clad twenty-something women sashayed over with sudden interest. They wanted Bertrand to show them where to put their hands and fingers, too. Bertrand nodded with a calm, experienced look. Julio laughed and gave Bertrand a wink but kept up the packing. Julio saw me watching the scene unfold.

"That Bertrand," Julio said. "He is a god."

I said, "A chick magnet."

Bertrand thanked the ladies for their interest, cordially excused himself, and returned to Julio. They took a load of equipment across the beach toward the parking lot. A couple of muscle-toned men offered their help. When the beach was clear of any traces of the demonstration, Bertrand and Julio came into the restaurant. With a big wave to the bartender, they hunkered down into a communal picnic table. Suddenly, the beach music coming through the speakers changed to "I Love Mud." Bertrand and Julio stood and graciously took a bow.

Olive and I corralled ever-shy Brie to the same table. Once Brie introduced herself, she and Bertrand and Julio discussed water purification, how many employees the plant required, and what percentage of the local taxes went to pay for it all. She was in heaven. Olive and I practiced being polite.

When a waiter placed two ice-cold beers in front of Bertrand and Julio, conversation stopped briefly.

A couple of police cruisers rushed by on the beach road.

"What a shame," I said. "Someone is having a bad day. I wonder where the cruisers are going."

Bertrand craned his neck to look in the direction of the police cars. "They are heading toward one of the gated communities."

He swung his attention back to us and looked me square in the eye. "The Simone family lives up there. And yes, I remember you."

Chapter Sixteen

Bertrand looked down at the table and took a breath as he brought his head back up. "You were at the sad event when Isabelle died, and you were at the casino when Donna displayed such unprofessional behavior."

"You went through school with Isabelle. Do you live in that area, too?" I asked.

"No," Bertrand said. "I grew up in a less posh community, although it was very nice compared to many. My father is an engineer, hence, I am an engineer. My mother is a jewelry artist."

"You grew up surrounded by beauty and brains. Lucky you," Olive said. "So you became a science guy and you perform musically. Is your music a good counterpoint to the science?"

"Because of my parents' hard work and success, I was able to go to science camps as a child and then the university. The singing and dancing were pure fun—and competition—for me." He shook his head. "That Isabelle, she was something. She was my major competitor in math and science. Of course, I never told her that, but she knew she was smart."

He looked thoughtful. "I will never be the performer she was, but I had fun playing the role of the tall, masculine island man just to agitate and, I think, motivate her," he continued. "She was pure joy and raw emotion to watch. So natural with the audience and generous with other performers. Isabelle appreciated hard work and commitment." Bertrand quickly looked out at the ocean, took a breath, and kept looking. He turned his head back to our table and took a swallow of his beer.

"Will you perform alone now, or at all, or maybe with another singer?" I asked. "You seem to have such an ease with the audience. Do you know what will happen with Isabelle's band and dancers?"

Bertrand shook his head, looking down at the table. "I have no idea, and other than the friends I have who depended on the work with Isabelle and what they have lost, I don't care." He corrected himself. "I care, but I don't want to be involved with it. Isabelle will be remembered for all that she was." His face turned more serious. "If someone attempts to step into her place, I think that person will be sorry. No one can simply step into Isabelle's place and expect all that Isabelle had earned. Ahh," he waved his hand as if to swat it all away. "Never mind."

Brie piped in, "Well, enough of this topic. It's time to eat, relax, and enjoy this day. I hope you don't mind sharing the table." She glanced at Bertrand and Julio. "Maybe we can talk about something else for a while and give Bertrand a break." She looked directly at Olive and me with eyes a bit wider than usual and held us in her gaze for a second longer than necessary.

We got the message. Brie; not so subtle sometimes.

"Well, whoever is up the road and having a hard time right now, we can send good vibes their way," I said. We turned our attention to food.

The chalkboard menu hanging on the wall behind the bar listed a variety of fish, fruits, and breads. Brie ordered a salad of mixed greens with mango, papaya, and pineapple chunks under a smoked yellow-fin tuna filet, topped with feta cheese crumbles and shredded toasted coconut. The vinaigrette dressing was cold and included basil and mango. Brie's first bite ended her conversational contributions. All we heard from her was an occasional "Mmmm, this is so good."

Several beachgoers and their children stopped by to speak with Bertrand and Julio. Known for their outreach from the water department, they were recognized by many children from their presentations in schools. Bertrand and Julio were gracious and friendly. Eating was secondary to socializing for them.

Olive and I shared a salad with mixed greens, quinoa, black beans, mango, papaya and pineapple chucks, avocado, and grilled shrimp slightly seasoned with smoked paprika and fresh grated ginger. It was light. It was cold and crisp. The ginger touched off a spark of heat.

The warm, mild wind kept flies away and the sweat on our arms to a minimum. The music was happy and the lyrics were carefree. Everyone was smiling, laughing, and enjoying themselves.

A uniformed officer walked through the beach area, scanning the crowd before stopping to talk with the bartenders, wait staff, and bouncers. Bertrand gave him a nod of hello, and the officer came to our table. Brie immediately gave Olive and me a glare of warning. Olive and I immediately exchanged glances of sheer delight and thoughts of further adventure.

"Good afternoon, Officer Michaud, and what brings you to a beautiful Saint Martin beach in uniform? You should be in swim trunks playing volleyball," Bertrand joked.

"There has been a break-in at one of the residences," Officer Michaud answered. "This is the closest public area to the residence. It would be a good place to blend in, so a few of us are taking a look for anyone who might stand out."

Bertrand said, "I haven't seen anyone suspicious-looking." He nodded toward us, the American tourists, and smiled at the officer. "Not like in the American movies where the thief carries a big black sack and the candlestick pokes through the top of the bag, eh?"

Officer Michaud laughed. "I see what you mean, Bertrand. Those American police have it easy. You want to catch a thief? Just look for the guys with the big black sacks. And don't forget the black hat. That must be part of the bad guy costume." We all chuckled.

"And what do your bad guys wear here?" I continued the joke. "Do they stuff the stolen property into their hats? Some of the headgear I've seen looks pretty big."

"You would be surprised at how much a resourceful thief can strap to his torso and hide under a dashiki. Those loose-fitting shirts cover all sorts of things. And they leave arms and legs free to run and scale walls when we chase them. None of that happened today, though. We got the call from the owner's wife when she returned home late this morning. She was frightened."

"What was the address?" I asked.

"You'll have to watch the news tonight for that," the officer smiled, held Bertrand's gaze for just a moment, gave a nod, and walked away.

"Well," I said, "desperate people do desperate things." I stabbed a piece of papaya. "I'm relieved no one was physically hurt, but having a home broken into must be scary. That poor woman must feel vulnerable, especially since they live up there in the more protected area."

Bertrand excused himself from the table and went in the direction of the officer. Julio finished his lunch while Olive and I savored the dessert we had saved room for.

It was a light-as-a-cloud French cream puff filled with raspberry sorbet and topped with drizzled fudge sauce. Oh yeah, this was heaven. If I was going to die anytime soon, this would make a great send-off. Brie treated herself to a spoonful of our sorbet as she sambaed away in a sorbet-induced cloud.

Julio entertained Olive and me with stories. He worked in the outreach department of the water plant. He teamed up with Bertrand once in a while. The outreach programs provided demonstrations inland in freshwater spaces, too. They taught children and adults how the plants and animals around and in water gave them important information about the health of the waters on and around the island. Of course, Julio had to make it fun and interesting for all ages. He was a certified teacher who preferred this type of teaching over the permanence of a school building. He and I talked about education on the island and learners with special needs.

Olive excused herself for a trip through the gift shop.

When Julio and I finished our conversation, he excused himself and went looking for Bertrand. It had been a solid half hour after eating, and the water was calling my name. Actually, it was Olive and Brie calling me.

How did they get into the water before me? Oh, of course, it was while I reapplied sunscreen and zinc oxide to my nose, cheeks, and shoulders. I continued to deal with enough skin cancer from all of those vacations at Happy Hampton Beach in New Hampshire in the sixties. I didn't need more.

This water was the perfect temperature for me. I walked right in up to my knees then to my thighs. In an instant, I dove underwater and scooted along, holding my breath, doing my best mermaid act. I surfaced and flipped my three inches of hair backward like a dramatic beach bunny that sent about five glistening drops of water into the air. I looked like a supermodel in my mind.

I swam over to Brie and Olive, who were treading water and smiling. Brie decided to swim the length of the beach as if she were seriously exercising. Olive dog-paddled and then floated around. I headed out to the floating platform.

I wasn't huffing too badly when I reached the ladder on the side of the float. It was about four feet high. Hauling these 125 soaking-wet pounds out of the buoyant, salty water took some serious pulling with my arms and pushing from my legs, which I would feel later. It was a clear reminder that I was indeed not one of the youngsters already running and jumping off the platform.

A line was forming behind me. Energetic kids waited for me to haul my tuchus up that ladder so they could scurry up and jump off all over again.

"Okay, I can do this," I positive-coached myself.

"Errgghh," I pulled up with my arms and pushed with my legs. I was up onto the bottom rung of the ladder! I was sure this was how one felt at the summit of Mt. Everest.

Then, suddenly, I felt it. Oh no, was that a cramp in the arch of my right foot? No, no, no. I couldn't fall back into the water without taking a couple of kids with me because they were right up behind me. Oh, oh, my big toe was curling up and the last two small ones were curling down…oh no…around the rung of the ladder. The pain was shooting through my foot and up my ankle. I was starting to panic and at the same time starting to laugh hysterically.

"Pardon, madam," said the boy right behind me, looking for a way around me.

This was a moral, ethical dilemma. Raise my cramped foot out of the water and show this preteen my condition to garner some compassion? Or, by the impatient look on his face, should I raise it and kick him in the shoulder, making it look like a muscle spasm, sending him off the ladder as a message to the kids behind him?

No, I self-talked, I will maintain my dignity. I have integrity.

I raised my arthritic-looking foot high enough for others to see it. That gave me a couple of seconds and I continued climbing. All thirteen rungs.

I moved onto the platform and before I could flop down to massage my foot, three of the kids from behind me had already raced across and off the platform. An American-looking man of about my age with a paunch over his plaid swim shorts eyed me and immediately understood my plight. He had a small cooler next to him. No joke. He had swum out here with his towel and cooler. He opened the cooler, fished out a couple of ice cubes, and handed them to me to rub over my cramp. Instant relief.

"Thank you," I sighed.

"*De rien,*" he murmured.

He wasn't American at all. He was French and oiled up to the point I wondered if he might slide off if the platform dipped too much to one side.

I rocked my foot back and forth on the floor of the platform and the cramp subsided. You know those next few minutes after a foot cramp when you don't dare move in case it comes rushing back? That was me.

By now, I had been in the sun for several minutes, and my joy was starting to wane. I rolled onto my hands and knees to stand up on the swaying platform and toddled over to the waterslide.

Waiting my turn in line, I had to put one hand on the teenager in front of me to keep my balance. Thank goodness this kid had a kind heart. Listening to his beautiful French, I understood something about his *grand-mere*. He smiled at me when I looked at him apologetically.

I was dry by now, and the climb up this ladder was much easier than the first one. I climbed and sat at the top of the slide. There was water flowing from jets on both sides, so the trip down would be slick and quick. I looked for Brie and Olive so I would have witnesses. Olive was under an umbrella on the beach; she waved. Brie was floating in the water; she stood up and gave me two thumbs-up.

I pushed off.

"Yee-haw!"

I flew down that slide and sailed off the end. For the moment I was airborne, the excitement felt like a jolt of electricity running through me. Then I was underwater flailing like a drunken octopus. I rallied and attempted my best Olympic diving return to the top. My frog-leg kick resulted in my bony ankles clanking together hard enough to leave a bruise. Swinging my outstretched arms firmly down by my sides to streamline my approach to the top didn't work well, either. One hand slipped off my thigh and just kept swishing by the front of me, causing all kinds of resistance to the water. It was probably for the best that there were no underwater cameras rolling. Greg Louganis would have been disappointed. But gosh, it was fun.

I swam back to Brie, who applauded my adventure.

"I would give you a ten!" she laughed. "You wanted to do it and you did it. Good for you. You looked great up there." Always the cheerleader.

We sloshed out of the water and rinsed off under the outdoor showers. Olive had already cleaned up and changed back into her clothes. Brie and I changed with the remaining tour mates, and we started loading into our van.

I settled into a window seat in front of Olive. "There's Bertrand getting into his water district car. Is that Donna walking across the parking area carrying a beach bag?"

She had full-length wind pants on and a skimpy beach top with a floppy hat and sunglasses. Not the celebrity look we had seen before, but everyone has downtime and days without makeup. She was smart to take a day to relax.

She saw our van and noticed us watching her. She abruptly veered over to an empty parked car. She shuffled through her bag, searching for her keys, but Olive and I had seen her walking from the road, not from the beach or bar.

"That isn't her car, is it? Why would she have left her car at the beach and walked down the road?" Olive asked.

"What's that in her beach bag?" I asked. "It looks hairy. I hope she isn't one of those twenty-somethings who carry their teacup dogs around in their purses. In this heat, no wonder it isn't moving."

Our van pulled away before Donna found her car keys. Maybe Bertrand would help her.

Chapter Seventeen

Bart drove us northward on this friendly island. Food, drink, sun, and swimming had relaxed us. We were quiet while Priscilla pointed out more of Saint Martin's highlights as we came upon them.

Riding along, rubbernecking to see the flora and fauna, I began to feel the sand and salt my quick shower had left behind. Miniscule irritants lined the leg elastic in my underpants, and sand between my toes itched just a bit, enough to distract me. Brie's head lolled onto my shoulder when her siesta time hit.

I heard Olive behind me.

"Okay, Google, warm coconut soup recipe."

I knew she was in her glory. A new soup recipe was the best souvenir she could bring to her daughter.

Priscilla alerted us that we were going through Grand Case, the French restaurant section.

"Olive," I said, "this is where Tastevin Restaurant is. I hope we can go there for lunch tomorrow. Eating on their balcony over the water is like living in a postcard."

I nudged Brie awake so she could see the changes in the area.

When we first came here a decade ago, side roads were dirt and now they were paved. There were more restaurants, and the time-tested, successful ones had undergone facelifts. The sidewalks had been renovated from broken concrete and loose bricks to smooth and modern-looking walkways.

"The area has come into its own," Brie said. "Nice." She went back to sleep.

It wasn't much of a jaunt from the Grand Case to Marigot, the capital and port. As we rode along the curving roads, Priscilla turned in her seat and flicked on her microphone.

"Marigot is where you come to shop, shop, and shop some more," Priscilla said. "The finest shops of Gucci, Versace, and Cartier are here. Whether it is clothing, perfume, or diamonds and other gems, you will find it here in Marigot. For those who want to round out their buying, the open-air market, very similar to the one in Phillipsburg, is here. Spices, vegetables, meats, and clothing are available from the many vendors. Be ready to haggle over prices. That is part of the experience. You can enjoy the music from the nearby bistros. Oh look," she gestured. "Do you see that couple dancing in the plaza? Make your memories of Saint Martin your own way—dance when you feel like dancing; sing when you feel like singing."

I was watching people as we rode by them. I noted their size, shape, and how they held themselves. I made up stories from these fleeting glimpses into their lives. It was a pleasant surprise that everyone stood tall and proud. What a difference being in the majority can make.

Substituting a beach towel for my shoulder, I shifted Brie's head onto the backrest of her seat. I leaned back and turned my face toward the window so I could tell my story to Olive and not disturb others.

At a stoplight, I pointed out the window.

"That six-foot-tall, egg-shaped woman disciplines her rich black hair into a bun atop her head to add inches and power. Her five-inch double-hoop gold earrings tickle her neck, and she likes that. She's telling anyone who looks, 'This is my island. This is my turf.'"

"Oh! I love that," Olive said.

"Her royal-blue, teal, and yellow horizontal-striped tank top ends just below her hips and leads to her banana-yellow fitted skirt that ends just above her fleshy knees."

I had to whip around in my seat to take more of her in when the light changed. I was mesmerized by this woman. "Her flat leather sandals are teal with royal-blue and yellow beads bouncing off their rawhide tethers. Her name is Jewel, and she's my friend and neighbor. Jewel's grocery bag, dangling off one arm, holds a baguette, a tin of sardines, and a liter of good scotch. She cools herself with the teal and yellow fan in her other hand. She's dressed to impress, but one of her secrets is that Jewel dresses to impress Jewel."

And then she was gone from sight, but my story went on. "Jewel works in an office, doing more than expected without being recognized for it, but she's okay with that. Jewel walks with confidence and a serene look. We share morning coffee at the café near her office and my writing studio. Jewel adds color to my life."

Olive looked at me. "That was amazing. I want to be friends with Jewel, too."

"Ooh wait, who is that?" I said, looking out the window again. Someone was walking in a hurry with their hood up—in this heat! The bill of a baseball cap stuck out, shading already sunglasses-covered eyes. The person wore a gray T-shirt and long, black, baggy shorts. Wait a second.

I sang "One of These Things" from *Sesame Street*. This person's attire did not fit in with everyone else's.

"Did that guy just get dropped into this tropical picture? Did he not get the memo on Caribbean youth attire? He looks like one of our disgruntled city youth from Portland. He must be basting in his own juices in all those dark clothes."

"You assume it's a guy," said Olive with a sparkle of fancy in her eye. "It's a girl." She began her own story. "And she may not be disgruntled at all, Miss Stereotype/Profiler. Angel, that's her name. She's coming home from the boxing ring where she just finished working out."

We passed her. Olive finished her story. "Imagine how muscular those legs were? Why, any second now, she could whip off that hood and cap and a Diana Ross-like Afro could explode from underneath."

"Ooh," I said, "I like your story better. Isn't it interesting how we can see the same thing but perceive it so differently?"

"Oh!" shot out of Olive's mouth, sitting bolt upright. "Do you think what we saw of Donna in the parking lot of the beach was what we really saw? I mean, we saw her go to a car and assumed it was hers. What if it wasn't? You saw how fast she turned toward that car. I thought she may have forgotten where she parked. But add that quick turn to her seeing us watching her, and add in that she was coming from the road, not the beach or bar. Ooh, the plot thickens!" she said, rubbing her hands together and smiling.

"That's good, Olive," I said. "That adds a lot to our theory. I can't wait to see Detective Poissonier."

"Hell no," announced Brie, sitting up. "You two are not going to see or talk with Detective Poissonier. Don't even think about it. She wants us gone. Doesn't that tell you enough, warn you enough, to keep your storytelling to yourselves?"

"Did you have a nice nap, Brie?" I asked. Sometimes being considerate will distract Brie from her point, and I hoped this was one of those times.

"Nap, shnap. With you two creating life stories of the people we pass on the street? No way, but I was enjoying your flights of fancy until you started on the murder. We are done with that, remember? Detective Poissonier has it under control. She does not want your help."

"No," Olive said, leaning forward and speaking between the seatbacks, "but she might need it, Brie. She might not want it, but she may need it. See, Vidalia and I are an indispensable part of the team here. I would have thought you had already figured that out by now. You might be slippin'." The smirk on her face showed she was testing just how far we could cajole Brie.

"Not funny," Brie shot back, fighting a smile. Then, almost begging, she said, "I want the last couple days of this trip to be relaxing. I want to eat good food, drink good drinks, and listen to languages other than English. I do not want to go to the police station and worry about one or both of you ending up behind bars." She issued forth her most serious face. "Honest to God, I'll leave you here on Friday."

Brie's face was scrunched up with her "I'm serious" look, but we weren't buying it. There was the tiniest sparkle in her eye that told me she didn't actually believe she was getting through to us but she had to try.

"Right," I said. "We think this is a small island so every bit of information related to the Simones would be sent to Detective Poissonier immediately. What if Saint Martin is just like any other place where well-intentioned people don't get the information sent? What if Officer A thinks Officer B is sending it and vice versa? It doesn't get delivered in a timely manner?"

Brie raised one eyebrow, giving me her "I'm-not-buying-your-line-but-I'll-let-you-keep-going" look. I took that as encouraging. I sensed a toehold, so I kept going.

"How about this? If we happen to see the detective, we can tell her what we saw and heard. She may then do what she thinks is best with our vital info. We don't act pushy, yet we contribute the vital information."

"You keep calling it vital information. You don't know that it is," said Brie. "Calling it vital doesn't make it so. And it doesn't influence my opinion that you two should stay out of this investigation."

"Duly noted," I said. We sat back in our seats. Olive glanced at me between the seats with a satisfied smile on her face.

I looked over at Brie. She had a satisfied smile on her face, too.

I closed my eyes with a satisfied smile on my lips. Glad we got that all cleared up.

"The next big decision will be where to eat dinner tonight," I said.

"Let's have Coco decide," Olive and Brie said at the same time.

Perfect.

We snoozed until we arrived back home.

We got out of the van, sluggish from our restful ride. We thanked and tipped both Priscilla and Bart. Brie and I hauled ourselves to our apartment for showers and glasses of iced coffee.

Rejuvenated, we met Olive and Coco in the lobby. Coco was happy to choose a nearby restaurant, and the three of us were quick to agree.

We walked to a section where sidewalks and roadways came together at a sharp turn. We heard people talking but didn't see anyone. Cars, busses, and motorcycles went by with their noises but we could still hear conversation, and it sounded close by.

Coco pointed upward to a balcony, which was where the voices were coming from. A handwritten menu was tacked to one of the posts holding up the balcony. We climbed the narrow, worn wooden steps and came into the tiniest restaurant I'd ever seen. We had Brie ensure that this was a real restaurant and that tourists were welcome. We didn't want to intrude on a local hangout. The staff assured us that we were welcome. We sat on the balcony at one of their five tables.

After I emphasized how much of a gringo I was and how much I didn't like hot peppers, we asked them to bring us their three most popular dishes. We ordered a bottle of wine and three glasses. Olive had sparkling water with an iced-tea chaser.

It was the best food. There was tender, cut-it-with-a-fork chicken and beef, crisp vegetables, plantains, and sweet potatoes, some roasted, some mashed. There was a smooth and savory gravy and two sauces in small bowls on the side.

I could have thrown my face into my plate, it was so good.

You know when you eat beef stew with extra carrots or traditional New England boiled dinner or a good pot roast, how all the flavors blend together and you eat until you could explode? So you sit back and chat for a while, nibbling still, the entire time?

That's what this dinner was.

The balcony was open to the mugginess and heat of the night, but we didn't care. Brie chatted with the staff, translating little bits to us if they pertained to the food, but she was in her paradise. Her eyes danced. She gestured and emphasized words. She was in her own world.

Coco, Olive, and I were really happy for her and chatted in lower voices among ourselves. Coco couldn't tell us much about her medical conference at the dinner table, so Olive and I filled her in on our observations.

Coco was in agreement that we should tell Detective Poissonier.

That was the only time Brie broke away from her conversations with staff and locals. A quick scowl from her let us know she had one ear on us. We each blew her a kiss and waved her away dismissively.

What a memorable night. No dessert for us. We were full. We also knew we had ice cream in our freezers and we would be ready after our strenuous walk back. After all, it was easily a half block away.

We tottered our stuffed and happy selves back to our rooms with hugs and thanks for a great evening. In our apartment, I dished ice cream, poured a little more wine, and propped my feet up on the balcony railing, glancing from the television to the ocean view.

TV news was covering the break-in. It was the Simones' home. Eduardo Simone, Isabelle's father, looked reserved, still, and rigid, scotch in hand. His wife, Patience, took measured breaths, but her gaze jumped around the room as the interview went on.

"I don't know what the intruders were looking for." She paused and then muttered to herself, almost inaudibly, "Calm breath in and anxiety out."

She paused. "We don't think they took any of the valuables." Again, she spoke, slightly more intelligibly this time. "Calm breath in, anxiety out." She looked around the room. "A few picture frames were smashed." I watched her breathing slowly in and out.

"Why slash the guest bedroom mattress?" she asked no one in particular. She turned her head to one side and reminded herself, "Calm in, anxiety out." Not trying to keep the mantra to herself any longer.

"We are taking inventory. I didn't realize how many things we have until we started listing each one." Her voice drifted off with her attention as she gazed around the room.

The camera cut to the reporter. "Still reeling from the sudden loss of their only child, Isabelle Simone, the singer, dancer, and humanitarian, the Simone family now must cope with a break-in into what they believed, until today, was their safe haven. As you can see behind me, uniformed police officers, detectives, and forensic teams are gathering evidence that will assist in determining who chose this family, at this time, to wreak havoc. The investigation into Miss Simone's death last week during a fundraising performance for the St. Emiliani Orphanage continues, and we will switch to my colleague Arturo DeMinas at Police Central Station for an update on that. This is Xavier Gilbert, on the scene. Over to you, Art."

In a flash, we saw the lobby of the police station we had "visited" with Detective Poissonier.

"Thank you, Xav, and good evening, ladies and gentlemen. We are here at the office of Detective Pamela Poissonier, lead detective in the mysterious death of Isabelle Simone. We have requested an interview and status update but have not seen the detective as yet. Detective Poissonier has been seen around the island as the investigation continues. We have a little footage of her at the hospital visiting an employee of the orphanage who, we've been told, took a tumble on some stairs. We plan to ask if there is a relationship between Miss Simone's death and this employee."

"Loooook!" I tried to keep my voice down. "We're in the video clip at the hospital! See us leaving Esther's room with the detective? Oh my gosh, she is not going to be happy about that."

Brie sat forward in her chair and watched.

The reporter looked over at the office door. It didn't open.

"And here we have footage of the detective speaking with Bertrand D'Lamore in a parking lot outside the Peacock Resort Casino on the very afternoon of Isabelle Simone's funeral. We plan to ask if Mr. D'Lamore is a suspect. Mr. D'Lamore has not been seen performing since Miss Simone died in his arms."

"Look!" I may have jumped up and down a bit. "Do you see us?" I pointed to the screen.

There in the background of the video were the four of us. Brie sat back in her chair and sighed.

Again, the reporter looked over at the office door. Still not open.

"Man, Brie, this reporter is stretching his story until our favorite detective comes out of that office. The poor guy is starting to sweat," I said.

"No one has been arrested yet," Art continued. "We plan to ask if she is close to an arrest and how, if at all, she believes this break-in at the Simones' home may be related to Isabelle's tragic death."

Third time was the charm. Arturo looked once more at that office door just as it opened. Detective Pamela Poissonier walked over to the group of reporters. Her face looked tired and serious. I wouldn't want to cross her right now.

"Yeah! Here she is. My favorite detective of all time!" I cheered like a fan.

"She is the only detective you know, Vidalia," Brie quipped. She put her hand over mine and smiled. "I enjoy how much fun you have at the oddest things." She chuckled. "You're so weird."

I gave her my Cheshire cat grin.

My new best friend's face and shoulders took up the entire screen. About six microphones were inches away from her mouth.

"Good evening, members of the press. I am Detective Pamela Poissonier of the Saint Martin Police Force. Please allow me to read my statement before asking questions. We continue to investigate the death of Isabelle Simone. Multiple interviews are being processed. The autopsy report and forensic evidence are being reviewed. The investigation is ongoing. This afternoon's break-in at the home of Miss Simone's parents is being closely analyzed for any relationship to the death. As of this time, we have no evidence or information that relates the two events."

"I do! I do!" I said. Brie squeezed my hand. I chose to believe it was an affirmation of her adoration and joy in my exuberance.

Detective P finished her statement. "Our continued condolences go out to the family. Thank you. And now I'll take just a few questions."

Voices from behind the microphones called out questions.

"Detective, what is the relationship between the orphanage employee falling down some steps and the murder?"

"Uh-oh," I said. "She's going to bite his head off."

Detective Pamela's eyes flashed at the reporter and held him in her stare. "This investigation has not been deemed a murder. You should be very careful, sir." She held the stare for a second longer. I could almost hear a tail swishing between the legs of the reporter. "As for the employee, that visit was part of the investigation and I will not comment on it at this time. Next."

"Detective, is Bertrand D'Lamore a suspect? Why were you speaking with him outside the casino the day of the funeral?"

Detective Poissonier brought her hands up into the camera frame and rubbed them together lightly, palm to palm, fingers intertwining. She kept an even gaze at the reporter. "Miss Simone died in Mr. D'Lamore's arms. He was the last person she saw, the last person to be near her. Mr. D'Lamore may have information essential to this case."

"You idiot," I added.

"Shh," quieted Brie.

"That is all the time I have for you right now, ladies and gentlemen. Thank you for your time and interest." Detective Poissonier turned on her heel and was back in her office before anyone could ask another question.

"Hey," I said, "Detective Poissonier explained why she spoke with Bertrand, but she didn't say why she was at the casino instead of asking him to the station for questioning. She didn't answer why that day and time, did she? How did she know Bertrand was there?"

"And, quite frankly," I put one hand on my hip, "I don't know why none of the reporters asked about the four of us."

Brie clicked off the television and put the remote on the table. "No, she didn't. And no, they didn't. Just think what you and your sister will make of that tomorrow." She stood and took my hand. "Now why don't you take your wine out onto this wonderful balcony with me?"

I did.

"Breathe in this gorgeous ocean air." Brie had one hand around my waist. I stilled my mind, closed my eyes, and breathed. I lowered my head to the top of hers and wrapped one arm around her shoulder.

"Now," she guided, "fill your mind and heart with us, in the warmth and wonder of this island, and let it fill your dreams tonight."

"Oh, *mon cher, perfecto*," I murmured huskily. And did just that.

Chapter Eighteen

Our last full day in Saint Martin.

Coco's conference was over, and she could enjoy the day with us. A quick breakfast on the beach of fruits, granola, croissants, and café au lait set us off toward the resort's dock for a water taxi over to Marigot. After the skipper rearranged where we sat so the boat was balanced for weight, we set off. It felt as though we were going seventy miles an hour, but it was more like thirty-five. The wind made my face feel scrubbed clean. The ride took less than half an hour, and we sidled up against the public dock in Marigot. We could see the open market from there. Our varied weights and sizes required that we stand in the order the captain told us in order to keep us from tipping over. We tugged at our clothes while waddling and lurching off the boat. The captain repeated our time for return was four o'clock sharp.

The open-air market was bigger than the one in Phillipsburg or at least more spread out. Olive wanted to look for a pair of pants to go with her new scarf. I was ready to look for my own souvenirs, maybe some earrings and spices. Brie was just looking at everything with Coco.

We were at a stall with wrap pants. If the wind blows hard, your leg may be exposed by the ruffling of the unsewn outside pant leg. They were billowy and sleek at the same time. Olive was thumbing through them, looking for the right colors. There was every combination imaginable.

"Ah, madam, here we are again."

Olive stood stock-still for a millisecond. In that time, she tightened her grip on her day pack under her free arm and made one step away from the voice. Then she recognized it. Olive looked briefly down at the ground, took a breath, and turned to Adrien Bemuse.

"I am a lucky man to have another stolen, romantic moment with you."

"Stolen is right, mister," Olive parried back. "I am here with my family, and you interrupt our wholesome fun with your crazy talk. You are stealing valuable vacation time." She took a breath, cocked her head to one side, and looked around the market. "And what kind of romantic moment is this? An open-air market?"

He never took his eyes off hers. Adrien had an amused and patient smile. The game was on. As she paused for a breath, he took Olive's hand. She rolled her eyes but left her hand where it was.

His chuckle had a bit of a hungry rumble to it. Olive caught it immediately. She whipped up her "take caution" index finger. Adrien hooked it with his own, pulled her finger to his lips, and kissed her knuckle.

Olive doubled over laughing but didn't let go. Adrien pulled her upright. With her hands in his, he twirled Olive away and back toward him. Olive was a bit off-kilter.

"You are good, Adrien. Smooth. I think you've had practice with this sort of thing. Do you work for the Department of Tourism?"

I gasped. Brie looked away. Coco said, "Olive, be nice."

"No, I don't mean to be mean. Places with beaches hire sweet young things to surf and play volleyball so the tourists have something to photograph. At night they have clean-up duty of the beaches. Maybe Adrien was hired to sweep women of a certain age off their feet and into a harmless rendezvous à la *Shirley Valentine* or *The Bridges of Madison County*." She turned toward Adrien. "Adrien, I am having the best time with you, really, I am. It's just too much. Listen, we have plans to eat at Tastevin in Grand Case. And we must be back for the water taxi so I don't have time for this, although it has been a highlight of my trip."

Adrien hadn't moved or let go of her hands.

"Olive. We each have only this moment to live, and I choose to experience it." He held both of her hands and stepped back to admire Olive head to toe, then looked in her eyes. "Experience it all with you."

Olive picked up the gauntlet, looked him straight in the eye. "All right, then, let's do this."

Adrien finally blinked.

Olive reached into her day pack and drew out the scarf he had mysteriously paid for in Phillipsburg.

"I brought the scarf—thank you, by the way—and I want to find pants to go with it."

Adrien fingered the scarf, relishing the memory from earlier in the week. He looked into Olive's eyes and smiled. He took her hand and led her to a wildly colorful stall with double-decker rows of slacks and skirts.

"Bonjour, Margaret," he said. "This fine woman wants slacks to match her scarf. I know you will help her nicely."

"Bonjour, Mr. Bemuse, ladies." Looking at Olive, she launched into the sale. "What type of slacks are you looking for—drawstring, elastic waist, or wrap?"

And so it went until Olive found a sandstone and green pair of wrap pants.

She was about to pay for them when Brie brought a different pair for her to consider. Brie has a great eye for colors.

Adrien stood back, nodding his head at different options.

It came down to two pairs. Brie and Olive are both Librans, and if you know anything about that, you know they have trouble making decisions. Back and forth it went.

I recommended buying both pairs, and Coco agreed. As sometimes happens in situations like this, Olive decided she didn't want any slacks and gave them both back to Margaret before walking away in a mild huff of indecision.

Adrien's arms dropped to his sides in disappointment. He helped Margaret refold and replace items in her stall as we moved away from the market.

At times like this, it's best to go have a snack and let things settle. Olive rebounded quickly. After a few sips of her decaf iced tea, she said, "Sometimes things aren't meant to happen. We can go back to the stall and get a pair later. It was all just too much in the moment."

"It was too much, all right," Coco said and smirked. "You and Adrien might have actually had some fun!"

"Tssst," Olive warned her. We all chuckled at her expense.

We found ourselves in a different part of the market with book and art stalls. Brie looked at titles while the other three of us browsed the art. Glancing over to keep sight of Brie, I recognized the woman operating the bookstall. It was the woman from the bookstore in Phillipsburg; it was Isabelle Simone's aunt. I elbowed Olive and rubbed my hands together in anticipation. We walked close enough to hear the *tante* speaking in French.

Let me say, dear reader, that I love this woman I live with. Brie was holding a book open in her hands, seriously looking at the text. For several seconds. Never turning the page. She was eavesdropping for me! Aww!

Olive and I stopped in our tracks and backed away, not so subtly. We picked up paintings and sketches, peering over them at Brie and Isabelle's *tante*. The two chatted while Brie bought a book and walked over to us.

"Nice book store," she said when she joined us. "Nice woman. Is it time to head to Grand Case?" She gave us a look that brooked no questions. We kept our questions for later.

We hailed a cab and headed to our lunch reservation.

We got the table I wanted at Tastevin.

Sheer drapes lined the entrance to the balcony. We were over the water. It had those warm and clear shades of blue that tempted me to jump right in. The sun was shining with barely a cloud in the sky. The table was set with more glasses and goblets than I would ever know when to use properly, enough cutlery for several courses, and small dishes set on top of larger plates. All on a white linen tablecloth. I felt as though we were in a Martha Stewart holiday dining room.

"This is a reward for all of the hard work I've done in my life. This is my vacation. My release from responsibility. My pampering myself. And I am grateful to share it with the three of you." I raised my water glass to Brie, Olive, and Coco.

"Hear, hear," said Brie, raising her water glass in toast.

Clinking goblets all around. And then Olive couldn't stand it another minute. She had contained herself too long.

"Okay, grateful, vacation, pampering—good. Tell us what Isabelle's aunt was saying in the bookstall, Brie."

"It took me a few minutes to remember this woman from the bookstore and the news coverage of the funeral. I wasn't proud of myself, but I started listening to her conversation with the woman from the next stall. You know, I try to keep my language skills up, so listening to two fluent speakers was a great opportunity."

"Oh yes," Coco nodded. "You would have listened to any conversation given the chance, I'm sure." She gave a two-second pause, rolled her eyes, and hissed, "What did she say?!"

"Oh right," Brie began. "Isabelle's *tante* told the other woman that her brother's house had been ransacked by some 'coo-coo' who took nothing of value except a few of Isabelle's clothes. The guest bedroom mattress was slashed. Her brother was afraid everything on the computer had been downloaded."

Brie adopted the *tante's* voice and continued in English, "My brother is beside himself, I tell you. He looks his usual buttoned-up and reserved self, but he is coming undone. Grief will do that when there are unresolved issues. I saw a show about it on *Dr. Phil*. But I didn't think he had any issues with Isabelle. He was always so good to her."

She took a breath and waved a fly away. "It must have been someone who obsessed over Isabelle. Why else would someone break in and steal her clothing? And you know what else? The thief took diaries. His wife, Patience, has all these spiral-bound notebooks stored in plastic tubs in the basement. They took 1988. Coo-coo."

Brie sat back in her chair and sipped her water, quite happy with herself.

A waiter brought menus and the wine list. We quickly decided on a bottle of cold chardonnay for the three of us while Olive had her usual water.

Looking out over the shallow ocean, I saw a lone rowboat and fisherman. He was pulling up traps, storing his catch, then baiting and throwing the traps back into the water. This was the scene people saw on large posters in travel agencies and airports. Here I was actually seeing it. I didn't bother trying to capture it in a photo. I simply engraved it into memory.

"I can't help myself," I said. "I have to get the lobster. That man in the boat deserves my support. I just have to believe that I am eating his fresh catch. I will have the lobster special, whatever it is."

"As you wish, madam," the waiter said. "Today's lobster tail is flayed and filled with a scallop and shrimp stuffing."

I sighed and nodded approval.

"Me too," cooed Coco. "I don't get many opportunities for lobster where I live. Crabs we have aplenty."

Olive ordered a salad with Cajun-spiced tofu cubes, those tiny corn on the cobs, and green and black beans mixed with chunks of avocado, mango, and extra papaya. Brie had the fish of the day with oil, capers, olives, and raisins.

Two hours drifted by as we looked over the ocean, had refills on drinks, and lingered over our food. This was heaven.

We were mulling over the desserts when a package arrived at our table.

"Pardon me, ladies, but this package was delivered for a woman named Olive with a description of a scarf very much like the one you are wearing." He looked at Olive. "I trust this is yours." He handed the package with the note to Olive and walked away.

Olive looked at each of us. We each shrugged our shoulders to imply that we had nothing to do with whatever was going on. She opened the note, scanned it, and said, "Oh no."

Coco was first to put it together. "It's from Adrien, isn't it? Read the note."

Olive took a breath. "Olive, I may never see these slacks drape your curves, but perhaps you will think of me and what might have been. Amor, Adrien."

Olive sat back in her chair and gazed out at the sea, looked back at the slacks, felt her scarf, and breathed. "This has been the best."

Over dessert and coffee, we decided not to talk about Isabelle's murder investigation. This place was too glorious to taint with death. We marveled and chuckled over Olive's new scarf and slacks and what might have been.

We took a taxi back to Marigot just in time to catch the water shuttle back to the resort. After all of the fresh air and the water ride, I was ready for a nap.

Chapter Nineteen

"Wow! That was a terrific nap," I said as we all met in the lobby at six thirty that evening. We had all slept and showered, and seemed ready for our final night on the island. We piled into the car and headed out. There was a restaurant/bar on the beach right next to the airport. We took a table as close to the beach as we could get and still watch the entertainment.

Brie and Coco decided to walk over and grasp the chain-link fence at the end of the airport. Despite the large signs cautioning people against it, they wanted to join the other adventurers. The gusts from planes idling at the end of the runway and then thrusting for takeoff can blow people off their feet. It sends sand, umbrellas, and small objects flying. Coco and Brie thought that sounded like fun. Olive and I made the sign of the cross at them, called them stupid, and waved them on.

Olive went for a quick walk down the beach, toward the sunset, while I sat at our table with our drink orders, taking it all in: the two old birds with fingers wrapped around the chain link, facing the tail of a Delta flight ready for takeoff; Olive, sporting her new slacks and scarf, running along the beach. She held the ends of the scarf as the fabric blew behind her in the wind. Then she sat on the sand to watch the sunset. She looked like a meditation.

Coco and Brie came back after two jets had landed and three had taken off, spitting sand from between their teeth. They could feel it everywhere, and they sat a bit uncomfortably but grinned like two cats who had caught their canaries. Coco held out the bottom of her bra and tried to shake some of the sand out.

Then we heard Donna start singing! Dru was backing her up. Brie, Coco, and I felt like groupies, we had seen her so much in this single week. Donna was singing "Feelings." Being nosy, as I can be, I looked at others in the restaurant. I saw Mr. Simone at a table.

"Do you see who is here?" I asked Coco and Brie.

"Poor guy probably needs a night away from his life right now. He's taking good care of that scotch on the rocks," said Coco.

Brie noticed, "Is he staring off into space or boring a hole through Donna? He seems to be looking at her but, I don't know, he doesn't look right to me. Not that I am an expert on this man. We've only seen him on television, mind you."

"You're right, though, Brie. He doesn't seem to be seeing Donna. Ooh, maybe he is seeing his daughter," I said, using air quotes. "You know, one last time."

Donna took a break after only two songs and went over to Mr. Simone's table. She remained standing, her face had a tight smile. Mr. Simone was saying something to her. He looked serious.

A waitress brought drinks to their table. They looked surprised and bothered by them. The waitress nodded in the direction of a man at the next table. He was sitting back in his chair, legs splayed. A faded New England Patriots T-shirt, baggy shorts, and sandals. His beard looked about a day old.

"You two look like you could use a drink," he said. He raised his bottle of beer in toast. "To life, right? From its serene waters to its riptides. Put one foot in front of the other and walk on." He belched and finished off his beer, adding the empty to the other four on his table.

Donna and Mr. Simone tried to ignore this fellow. Mr. Simone continued talking.

Dru walked over to the table now. He bumped into the guy's foot in the walkway between tables. The two men looked at each other.

"I'm drinkin' to a lot of things," he explained to Dru. Then he finished his sentence singing Cole Swindell's "Ain't Worth the Whiskey." He was clearly nursing a busted-up romance.

Dru patted the guy's arm. "Funny, buddy. Easy does it."

As this happened, Mr. Simone stood on wobbly legs, at this point in his drinking. Donna had approached him with a thin, apprehensive smile. Now her shoulders were lowered in what might have been relief while Mr. Simone spoke to her.

He took an envelope out of his slacks pocket and held it out to Donna. Her face contorted into a horrific expression. Mr. Simone kept talking and pushed the envelope into her hands. He looked her straight in the eye, nodded, and turned to leave, holding tables and chairs to steady himself.

"Ooh, I think he gave Donna money to continue in his daughter's path. That's so sweet," I said.

Dru was with Donna at this point, holding her shoulders as if to steady her. She looked off for a second and snapped her face back to Dru. Her face was tight with control now.

I looked over the now-darkened beach for Olive. She was going to love this part of our story!

Olive was standing up, yelling at someone in the water, "No! No, you can't do that. Sir? Sir! You can't just walk into the water with all your clothes on!"

It was Mr. Simone, and he was not listening.

Olive ran over toward him. He was thigh-deep with the tide going out fast. The waves kept knocking him off balance, and he didn't fight to stay upright.

I had fought those waves myself, getting tossed down while trying to get out of the water.

Olive was looking around for someone to help. I thought to myself, she does not want to get her new clothes wet.

Mr. Simone got knocked down and didn't stand up. He rolled with the tide surging out.

I heard Olive say, "Oh man." She walked into the water. She wrapped her new scarf around Mr. Simone's arm and started dragging him toward land.

From out of nowhere, Detective Poissonier walked toward the water. Unbuckling her belt and dropping her holster on the sand, she entered the water. Mr. Simone started fighting his rescuers.

There are few things Olive detests more than a drunk. She was probably ready to drop him and let him get his due, but grace must have entered into her and she worked with Detective Poissonier until all three were far enough up on beach that Mr. Simone could be managed.

I heard sirens. Medics arrived and took the drunken, grief-filled man to the hospital. Olive returned to the table a wet mess.

"I can't catch a romantic break, can I? Look at me!"

You know that chortle that comes up through your nose when you're really trying hard to be compassionate with the person who is distraught? I was trying harder than that. I fought my lips to keep them in a straight line, but they kept turning into a smile. If you could have seen my sister, dear reader. She was a sight. From her wet, flat-against-her-head hair, to the clinging clothing she kept pulling away from her body and that sucking noise that goes with it, to her forlorn look.

The strand of seaweed hanging from her hair onto her shoulder was just too much. She really looked like something the tide had dumped and left behind. Olive gave me a warning look.

Too late.

I sputtered my chardonnay out of my nose and collapsed onto the tabletop. Brie had gallantly gone for napkins from the bar. Coco was standing next to Olive at this point, tentatively patting Olive's shoulder.

"Come with me, Olive," Coco said, "I know what to do." She took my sister to the souvenir shop next door. Our Jane Wayne to the rescue.

They came back about twenty minutes later. Olive had used an outdoor shower to get as much sea off of her as she could. Then she had changed into her brand-new souvenir-shop top and skirt. Her sandals squeaked as she walked into the restaurant, and she was combing her hair dry. Our eyes met, Olive threw her shoulders back, and she strutted to our table. Coco was carrying the wetness in a mesh shopping bag, smiling.

"Well, that was interesting, wasn't it?" Olive remarked as she sat down. "This is one for the storybooks. My kids won't believe this is what their mother did on vacation."

A round of drinks was delivered. "We will have one of each of your appetizers, please," said Brie. "There will be something for everyone. They will each be delicious, and the wait will be short." She is so smart.

"This has been a vacation to remember, hasn't it?" I asked. We sat back in our chairs. The restaurant manager had put on recorded music. Donna was nowhere to be seen. Olive was shaking her head from all that she had been through when she said, "Uh-oh."

Detective Poissonier was walking toward us. She took in the four of us and hung her head in despair. She hadn't recognized Olive all wet and sandy in the fading light while they had been dealing with a near-drowned Mr. Simone. She raised her head to face us. Like any strong and resilient woman, she pushed her shoulders back, straightened her spine, and came to the table wearing a navy one-piece coverall.

"She must keep that in her cruiser," I said. Her hair was wet. She pulled a dry notepad out of her pocket.

"She must keep extras of those in her cruiser, too," Coco said.

"Ladies from Maine, we meet yet again. Exactly when will your time here in Saint Martin end?" the detective asked, not even trying to appear simply curious.

Olive took the lead. "We fly out tomorrow afternoon."

"Thank you for your assistance with the water victim." She spoke directly to Olive. "I am here to get some information from you. I hope we will not need to have you come into the station for a formal statement since we have so many witnesses. Please take me through what happened."

"I was relaxing on the beach. I had watched the sunset and was thinking over this vacation when I saw this man walk into the water. He was fully dressed, for crying out loud. Shoes and everything. I didn't see where he came from. When the wave knocked him over, I knew he was in trouble. I kept thinking his family or friends would come and get him. When that didn't happen, I yelled at him, but he kept going in deeper. I don't know if he heard me or not, but he was getting deeper into trouble. So I went in after him. Then you came, thank God." Olive shook her head. "I can't believe it all happened. Will he be all right?"

"So you did not see Mr. Simone until he entered the water where you were sitting?" the detective asked.

"It was Mr. Simone? I didn't recognize him. It was him? Oh, that poor, poor man. I thought he was a drunken tourist."

"Yes," I interjected, because that's the kind of helpful person I am.

"Mr. Simone was here at a table watching Donna and Dru perform," I continued. "Then Donna spoke with him. He was wobbly when he stood up, and the three of us noticed that he didn't seem right. But he said something to Donna that made her happy then shocked, maybe devastated. He handed her an envelope and teetered out of the restaurant."

Coco added, "Some guy ordered them drinks and made some toast to life. After Mr. Simone left, Donna pulled herself together faster than anyone I have ever seen, and in nursing I see a lot of people go through all kinds of emotions. Donna was distraught one second and in full command the next. Dru was with her. Then Olive started screaming and broke us out of the drama at the table and out onto the beach. After the EMTs left, Donna and Dru were gone."

She added, "We got Olive rinsed off and into these very fine togs." She waved her hand up and down Olive like a game-show hostess. "If you have a few minutes, we are about to share some appetizers, Detective. C'mon and join us. Think of it as a farewell celebration."

"Besides," I said, "we have other information you may be interested in." I purposely did not look at Brie. This wasn't exactly according to our agreement that Olive and I would share our observations only if asked, but with all that had happened that night, what the heck.

Olive was back into the story, our theory of what was happening in this murder case.

"We were at Orient Beach when the Simone home was broken into. When we got into our tour van, Vidalia and I saw Donna."

Detective Poissonier exhaled and dropped into a chair.

"She walked into the parking area from the road, not the beach," Olive continued. "We thought that was odd, but we don't know where Donna lives or what else is nearby on that road. She was dressed in workout clothes, I'd say. You know, wind pants and an exercise top. She was carrying a bag. We figured it was her clothing. She didn't have any makeup on, and she had big sunglasses on. I imagine she gets recognized a lot on the island, poor thing."

The detective had begun writing furiously.

"We felt badly for the small dog she had in her bag because it was so bloody hot. It wasn't moving. We feared the dog was dead from the heat." I paused. "So we were staring at her and she caught us. The cost of celebrity, eh? They can't have a minute to themselves without people like us gaping at them. So she turned to her car and was fishing out her keys from her bag, but she didn't find them before we drove away."

Olive added, "I remember thinking that it wasn't her car. That maybe she turned to the closest car she saw just to get us to stop gawking at her."

"Yes," I agreed. "We just wanted to tell you all of that, in the event that it might be useful. I'm sure your police officers at the beach that afternoon saw her and included it in their report." I added that at the end hoping we weren't about to get yelled at, locked up, or escorted from her island.

"Ladies, thank you for your help and observations. I am going back to the station for a shower and to file this report. I hope you have a smooth flight home. The next time you decide to visit the Caribbean, think of our many lovely islands before you choose. Goodbye."

"That was the nicest brush-off I've ever gotten," Coco said.

Chapter Twenty

"*Au revoir, et merci*, Peacock Beach Resort!" I hollered, waving as we drove away. Our bags were tucked into the trunk, and we were dressed for travel. I wouldn't give up my sandals until I had to. My sneakers and socks were stuffed into an outside pocket of my suitcase for a quick change at check in. I'd already submitted to long pants, but I was wearing a tank top. My long-sleeved shirt was tied around the strap of my day pack. My turtleneck was in the bottom of that pack. I would put that on over my tank top when we laid over in Charlotte.

It was good to have a plan.

"I see why you and Brie like to come here," Olive said to me. "It's the perfect weather. The people are so nice, and don't get me started on the food. I have never eaten so much mango in my life. Papaya is my new favorite fruit."

"Yes," chimed Coco, "this heat is a killer for me, but my body has loved the fresh fruit every morning. It's hard to come by in Alaska." She continued, "I've really enjoyed being on Saba Island at the medical school. It's amazing—a modern facility built on an island where engineers from around the world said it would be impossible to even build a road. Well, they did it! It's like no other facility I've seen."

Brie was looking out the car window, memorizing the sights.

"I love how easy it is to drive around this island," I said. "I could live here."

"Easy for you," said Brie. "Your Massachusetts driving skills all come out when you're here. These rotaries scare me to death."

We arrived at Princess Julianna Airport, dropped off the rental car, and started looking for our airline to check in. You know what a typical airport scene is like. Hordes of people in all shapes, sizes, and colors looking as though they know exactly what they're doing. And then there was us, stumbling through our own comedy of errors. First we went one way—nope, that was for arrivals. Now that way—oh, the serpentine line for departures.

On our third pass, our e-tickets negotiated from one of those irritating kiosks, we headed over to the actual human who would take our luggage and ship it straight through to Boston. We kept our eyes on one another. We knew about women going missing. We were giddy and giggling when who should sashay by but Donna.

And oh, what a sight. In a linen pencil skirt with a bolero jacket and five-inch heels. A cuff bracelet matched her earrings. Her outfit said, "I'm a serious woman and know how to use everything I have—I've got this."

Donna had an entourage of half a dozen people following her, including Dru. She was talking on her cell phone as she walked at a brisk clip. The smallest bit of moisture on the tiled floor and she was going to go flying.

"Hi, Sam, sweetheart. I'm just confirming the performance tonight on Saint Lucia. We're at the airport now." There was a small hesitation as if she had been interrupted. Her voice was a bit louder when she resumed.

"We are at the airport, yes. I expect Bertrand to fulfill his commitment to keep this local leg of the tour." Another pause. She had slowed her walk now, and her voice became louder and rougher. She came to a full stop before exclaiming, "Why would you cancel the tour? I can pick it up and carry it through. At the start of every show, we'll give a little nod of sorrow and get on with it."

Another longer pause. I appreciated the break so we could edge closer to catch every word.

"Sam!" Donna was sounding shrill. "You know Isabelle and I were interchangeable. She is gone, and now it's my turn."

Another pause.

"You listen to me," Donna lowered her voice, "my troupe and I are boarding the next flight to Saint Lucia. The rest is up to you. I don't care if you cancelled prematurely—we are professional performers and don't plan on letting our audiences down. We are headed to the venue now. Just make it happen, Sam," she barked. "Do your job. No one is indispensable."

Donna dropped her phone into her Gucci bag and huffed.

Dru said something to her.

"Shut," she glared at him. "Up."

"I told you I would take care of everything, and I am. Don't start with me."

The troupe members exchanged worried looks.

Donna approached the desk at check-in with a demure smile and began talking with the clerk.

"What? The no-fly list!" Donna's hands came down on the countertop with a slap. She dug her phone out.

"I guess Sam is suddenly needed again. He may not be as dispensable as Donna thought a second ago," I chirped.

"I demand satisfaction!" Donna yelled. "You put me on an effing plane now!"

Security people started to get closer. A uniformed woman stepped up to Donna and began speaking with her in a low and calming voice.

"Calm down, you say?" she continued yelling. "Not a chance, sister. Either get me on a plane or get out of my way."

Her eyes flitted around the area. She realized she had an audience. During her second sweep, she saw all of the uniformed officers.

Coco assessed, "She's one of those people who believe being loud gets you what you want. She's about to learn a valuable life lesson, I think."

"Fine, I'm leaving, but I'll be back," she snapped at the clerk. She started walking with a determined look on her face toward the exit.

The four of us and many others were watching and listening to this event unfold. "We won't need an in-flight movie after this," Coco said.

Like a barometric pressure drop before a big storm, it became quieter. Conveyor belts stopped. We looked around. I noticed the high number of TSA officers. Then, just like in the movies, Detective Poissonier burst through the double doors from outside flanked by officers in Kevlar vests and helmets. Rifles drawn. Everyone froze—no one needed to be told.

The detective walked directly toward Donna. The clerk took a step back from her console. Donna's crew stood with hands by their sides so officers could see they held nothing in them.

"Belladonna Fleur," began the detective, "put your hands where I can see them."

Slowly, Donna raised her hands, phone in one hand, handbag dangling from the other.

"Ooh, she looks like a cornered animal," Brie said.

"You are under arrest for the death of Isabelle Simone; for the attempted murder of Esther Stephenson; for breaking and entering; for destruction of property; and for theft and terrorizing. You have the right—"

Donna's eyes went wild with indignation. "I have the right? To what, Detective? I have the right to continue my tour. That's right, my tour. Isabelle is gone, and I am taking over what is rightfully mine."

Detective Poissonier continued, "You have the right to an attorney. If you cannot afford one, a lawyer will be appointed to your case."

"How dare you," Donna spat. "Daddy will take care of all of this indignity. And he'll take care of you, too."

Out of the corner of my mouth, I asked Olive, "Who is Daddy?"

"Tssst!" she whispered back. Then, "I'm getting a bad feeling about this." She looked at Donna with her eyes slightly pinched as if concentrating on something. She whipped her head back to me and said, "Oh my goodness, I think I know!"

Brie's eyes glided smoothly over to the two of us. It was a warning shot. Some might describe it as a glare.

"You have the right to remain silent," advised the detective. "Anything you say may be used against you in a court of law."

"Court of law?!" growled Donna. "Where was that court when my father got my mother pregnant and then refused her? Daddy tossed her away like a used tissue." She wept.

"Oh, she is coming apart at the seams. Are you seeing these emotional spikes and plummets?" Coco said. "I almost feel sorry for her."

"Do you understand these rights as I have explained them to you?" Detective Poissonier asked.

"Oh, I understand all right," sneered Donna. "Do you, Detective?

Do you? Do you understand that my last name should be Simone, that Isabelle and I are half-sisters?"

Donna took a breath. "You want to arrest someone? Arrest Esther. This is all her fault. It was that old bat who decided to let my father slip away from his responsibilities. My dark Haitian mother would have only brought embarrassing hardship to my light-skinned Brazilian father. Esther," almost spitting now, "Esther decided I was worth less than Isabelle. That day in the Records Room changed everything."

She nodded once and looked away for a second.

"I know who my parents were." She snapped her head back to face the detective. "I have rights. I have family. All I had to do was force Daddy to claim me as his. If Isabelle was close to death and I showed the family how I could step in and take care of her, Daddy wouldn't be able to deny me. If Daddy thought he might lose a daughter, he would see how valuable life is and welcome me with open arms." Donna's eyes were sparkling now.

"Magical thinking if I've ever heard it," said Coco.

Dru hollered, "Shut up, Donna! Wait for a lawyer."

"Shut up, you stupid, stupid man. You're the one who killed her. The belladonna was supposed to make her sick." She pointed her finger at Dru. "You are the one who cut her with that money. It was you who wanted Isabelle dead because you loved her, but she loved Bertrand. If you couldn't have her, no one would. Well, now you can go to hell with my sister. Bertrand and I can finally have the life we were destined to live."

Her eyes glowed with hope now.

"Your cut, Dru, gave the poison a direct path to Isabelle's bloodstream. She was already sweating from the skin contact of the belladonna I put into her costume. If you had just left it up to me, everything would have worked out, but now you've gone and ruined it."

Donna turned to the detective. "Detective, arrest this man for the murder of my sister." Two officers started to handcuff Dru. He was weeping and collapsed against one of the officers.

"I didn't know," he muttered.

Detective Poissonier said, "Take him away. We will get to him later. Now, Miss Fleur, hand your phone and bag to the officer next to you so I may handcuff you."

"No! No!" Donna shrieked. She threw her phone at one officer and swatted her bag at another. They each took an arm and "guided" them behind her back. Detective Poissonier put the handcuffs on.

"Take her in," she ordered. The two officers led Donna away while she shrieked and struggled. "He loved my mother, Celeste Fleur! He told me he always loved my mother!"

And then, it was all over.

TSA and airport staff resumed their work as if nothing had happened. Detective Poissonier lowered her head, exhaled a long breath, and then looked up and around.

And there we were, gob smacked, staring at her.

The detective lowered her head again, then raised it with her eyes closed. She opened her eyes and walked over to us.

"Bet she wishes she had some of that Rescue Remedy right now," Olive quipped.

"Hey, Detective P," said Coco, "you almost missed our leaving your island. Isn't this great! So nice of you to come and see us off." Coco giggled. "But seriously, sister, good collar there. Didn't see that coming."

"I did," I said. "Donna must have told her father that she knew she was his and had proof. That's what the hubbub was about at the funeral, wasn't it? That's what rocked Mr. Simone."

The dear detective gave me the blandest of looks. Then she smiled.

"After we transported Mr. Simone to the hospital, he began to ramble his thoughts aloud. He had acknowledged that Donna was his daughter during the pregnancy and birth. He had loved Celeste Fleur with all his heart but was married. His plan had been to keep Donna and her mother in an apartment. He would see them when he could, but they would want for nothing. When Celeste died during the birth, everything fell apart."

"I knew it. I knew it. I knew it!" I piped up. Olive gave me an elbow jab to the ribs.

Detective Poissonier continued, "The midwife took charge. Esther was from the old school where the class system was honored. Since then, Mr. Simone has been the benefactor for all of the dance and singing lessons, for the new dance shoes and costumes. He tried to give his second daughter as much as he could, given the situation."

"Guilt has a way of motivating us, doesn't it?" said Coco.

Detective Poissonier looked at her watch and the flight departure board. She continued, "He guided Isabelle to work with Donna and others at the orphanage. That gave him more reason to support the orphanage and get onto the board, so he could see Donna growing up. He watched his two daughters dance and sing together. They became close friends. It gave him glimpses of happiness and pride, but the terrible truth gnawed away at him."

"Well, I'll be dipped," I said. "The silver lining is that the truth is out now. Both the father and child are known to everyone. Maybe they can move forward together. Of course, with tons of therapy. If this doesn't sound like a great movie, I don't know what does."

The detective chuckled. "You and your stories. The two sisters in search of soup recipes, isn't it? And you get involved with the murder of the decade." She looked at Olive. "I took your advice, you know. I have Rescue Remedy in my car, in my desk, and at home. I think it helps. Thank you for that."

"You should take some right away," Olive replied. "Your body just went through a lot of adrenaline, and your muscles are going to cinch up. Go put a few under your tongue while you drive to the station."

Detective P. shook her head. "I'm not leaving until I see you through security and you are all on the other side, waiting at your gate."

"Well, Detective Poissonier," Brie said, "good luck with your neighborhood program. Officer DuBois told us about it. I plan to bring it up to our chief of police back home. I hope I can stay in touch and see how the program progresses. I think every town would benefit from it. Very impressive, Detective. Thank you."

"Your affirming feedback is what I need to hear right now. The team has been asked to present to the entire island force at the annual convention. That will be a big step." She checked her watch. "Now let's get all of you through security."

I headed up the group, and we meandered our way through the long line. We removed our shoes and set our bags in the tote bins. We raised our arms and walked through the X-ray screening machines.

As I put my shoes back on, I looked back to check on Brie and saw Detective Poissonier watching us.

Of course the alarm went off on Brie, of all people. The detective had a laser focus on her now. One eyebrow raised, she looked ready to leap into action to get us on the next plane off the island. In pure Brie form, she complied and thanked the officer who patted her down and waved the handheld metal detector over her chest and legs. She got through on her second pass.

All we had to do now was to locate our terminal and gate. This may sound straightforward, but remember who you're dealing with here. Coco needed a neck pillow for the flight. Brie had finished her books and needed a new one for the flight. Olive is always looking for souvenirs for family and friends. Me? I'm always ready for a snack. So we shuffled, close-knit, toward stores. After the purchases, we moved toward a bistro that sold snacks.

As we returned to our gate, our flight was called for boarding. And we did.

We read, drank, ate, slept, and chatted.

In Boston, we hugged Coco goodbye. Her flights would take her across our great country back to Alaska. We took the bus back to Portland, shoveled out my car, and drove home to Waterville. We dropped Olive at her house and went to ours.

Brie and I have our routine. The suitcases remained in the entryway, and we brought the laundry baskets down to them. Clothes went directly to the washing machine, and suitcases were stored in the furnace room. Everything else was put away. Wine was poured.

We sat and started to sort through all of the mail the cat-sitter had brought in but realized we were too pooped to do anything constructive. We looked through my phone at the pictures I'd taken.

"Hey," I said. "I wonder if the detective or the television station would send us a copy of those videos that we were in. Maybe I'll make some calls in the morning."

Brie closed her eyes and shook her head.

"Tomorrow, we'll go out to breakfast because we don't have any fresh food here. Then we'll shop for groceries. One of us will start the laundry, and one of us will put the food away. By then, we'll be ready for a nap."

Brie put her hands on either side of my head and looked me straight in the eye.

"Let's leave Detective Poissonier alone, eh? Think about it. She is in the middle of the hearings and court appearances. She doesn't need you on the phone. Let's just go to bed."

I put each of my hands on either side of her face.

I gazed lovingly into her eyes.

"Okay, let's just go to bed." I smiled and gently kissed her.

Walking toward our bedroom, I thought, Coco knows technology. She'll get those tapes.

Recipes

Olive's Pineapple, Papaya & Ginger Cooler

Ingredients
1 ripe papaya, peeled, seeded, and cut in cubes
1 cup pineapple chunks
3/4 cup pineapple juice
1 tablespoon lime juice
sprigs of mint
1 12-ounce bottle ginger beer or ginger ale

Put the fruits and juices in a blender and blend until smooth. Just before serving, add the ginger beer and pour into glasses. Garnish with mint if you like that sort of thing.

I served this at a women's group moon party, and they loved it! It is ice-cold, thick, and full of ginger depending how strong your ginger brew is. To tame it, use ginger ale.

Spicy Coconut Noodle Soup

Ingredients
1 can coconut milk (15 ounces)
2 cups roasted chicken broth (or water)
1 teaspoon ginger, minced
4 cloves crushed garlic
1 cup mushrooms, sliced
1 cup peas
1 tablespoon tamari or soy sauce
1 tablespoon agave or honey
6 ounces rice noodles

Instructions
Add the coconut milk, broth or water, and ginger to a pot. Bring to a boil over medium heat. Stir in the mushrooms, peas, tamari or soy sauce, and agave or honey. Reduce the heat and simmer for about 5 minutes until the vegetables are tender, stirring occasionally. Add any protein you like. I use cut-up chicken or shrimp. Remove from heat. Add noodles, cover, and leave it alone until the noodles are cooked as you prefer them.

This soup was the most perfect thing while I was under the weather. Niece Elizabeth brought me her original recipe, which didn't include any measurements. I added the coconut milk and measurements. If you like more garlic, ginger, or mushrooms, go for it.

Colorful Black Bean/Mango Soup

Ingredients
2 tablespoons vegetable oil
1 large onion, chopped
3 cloves garlic, minced
2 medium sweet potatoes, peeled and diced
2 large bell peppers: red, orange, and/or yellow, seeded and diced
1 15-ounce can diced tomatoes
2 cups vegetable stock or broth
1 15-ounce can black beans, drained and rinsed
salt and freshly ground black pepper
1/2 pound either chorizo or shrimp
2 ripe mangoes, peeled and diced. If you can't find fresh in your produce department, get a bag of frozen.
1/2 cup chopped cilantro or coriander, for garnish

Instructions
Heat the oil in a large saucepan over medium heat. Add the onion and chorizo or shrimp and cook, stirring often, for about 5 minutes until softened. Remove the chorizo or shrimp and set aside. I cut each shrimp into thirds to match the size of the fruit and veggies. Stir in the garlic and cook, stirring, for 3 to 4 minutes until the onion and garlic are golden.

Stir in the sweet potatoes, bell peppers, tomatoes with their juice, and vegetable stock. Bring to a boil, then reduce the heat to low, cover the pan, and simmer for 15 minutes until the sweet potatoes are tender.

Stir in the beans and simmer gently, uncovered, until they are heated through. Season to taste with salt and freshly ground black pepper. Stir in the mangos and chorizo or shrimp and cook until they are heated through, about 1 minute. Serve with cilantro if you like it.

I tested this recipe the day before a huge storm in December. Rosemary and I both loved it. We froze half of it for later in the winter.

Acknowledgments

My first piece was published in *Central Maine Today's Women's Quarterly*. I want to thank Terri Hibbard, Amy Calder, and Bridget Campbell for the supportive launch they gave my writing.

The Meetinghouse column in the *Portland Press Herald* has graciously printed over twenty of my pieces. To Greg Kesich and Sarah Collins, I cannot thank you enough for the ongoing support and encouragement.

My writing group has been with me every step of the way. Writing articles while learning how to write one, drafting and revising the outline for a book, and then writing each chapter has been nurtured and refined by Gale Davison, Kate Cone, Patricia Slater, Grace Von Tobel-Reed, Janet Murch, and Aren Givens. Meeting every other week has fueled my writing. There would be nothing printed in my name without you.

My main characters are near and dear to my heart. Deb Rich, Rosemary Winslow, and Tania Renfrew-Thomas live exaggerated lives in this book. Sort of.

Thank you, Verna Pierre for a great dinner where you shared your personal experiences and observations from living in Haiti. Thank you, too, to the staff at Eric's Restaurant in Waterville. You allowed me to take very long breakfasts to write much of this book longhand.

If you ever hear that I've expatriated, it will be to Saint Martin. I love everything about it. Rosemary and I have been there more than anywhere else. All of the places are real, and my intent has been to honor them.

Longtime friend and interpreting colleague Deb Gould escorted me on this publishing journey. Thanks, Deb.

Maine Authors Publishing & Cooperative, including Nikki Giglia, Nadia Kasperek, and the editing, design, marketing, and sales folks, is the force behind finishing my story and getting this book onto shelves. I appreciate what you do.

Fellow creative and terrific photographer Gale Davison took and unwrinkled parts of my face for the author photo.

Laura Landers created the fabulous cover illustration from phone conversations and shared sketches. Her question to me was, "What do you see as your cover?" She nailed it.

For all of my experiences, associations, and relationships, I am deeply grateful.

Jody Rich of Waterville, Maine

Jody Rich makes life decisions based on opportunities to travel, sing, and dance. She has gathered a brain full of people, places, and situations. Choosing from the many characters and adventures she has experienced, Jody crafts fiction that includes memoir moments. Her writings have appeared in the *Portland Press Herald* and *Central Maine Today*. Jody lives in Waterville, Maine, with her wife, Rosemary, and their cat, Lexus.